CLASSIC
MARVEL®
SUPER HEROES

CLASSIC MARVEL® SUPER HEROES

THE STORY OF MARVEL'S MIGHTIEST

BY PETER SANDERSON

becker&mayer! BOOKS

Library of Congress Control Number is available.

ISBN: 1-932855-56-4

Printed in China

Design: Todd Bates
Image Research: Kate Perry
Editorial: Conor Risch
Production Coordination: Leah Finger and Peter Schumacher
Project Management: Sheila Kamuda

10 9 8 7 6 5 4 3 2 1

becker&mayer! Books
11010 Northup Way
Bellevue, Washington 98004

www.beckermayer.com

CONTENTS

CAP, IN HIS OWN MAGAZINE AT LAST!
APPROVED BY THE COMICS CODE AUTHORITY
CAPTAIN AMERICA
MARVEL COMICS GROUP
12¢ IND.
100 APR
BIG PREMIERE ISSUE!

INCREDIBLE HULK
MARVEL COMICS GROUP
20¢
152 JUNE
02456
THE INCREDIBLE HULK
WHO WILL JUDGE THE HULK?

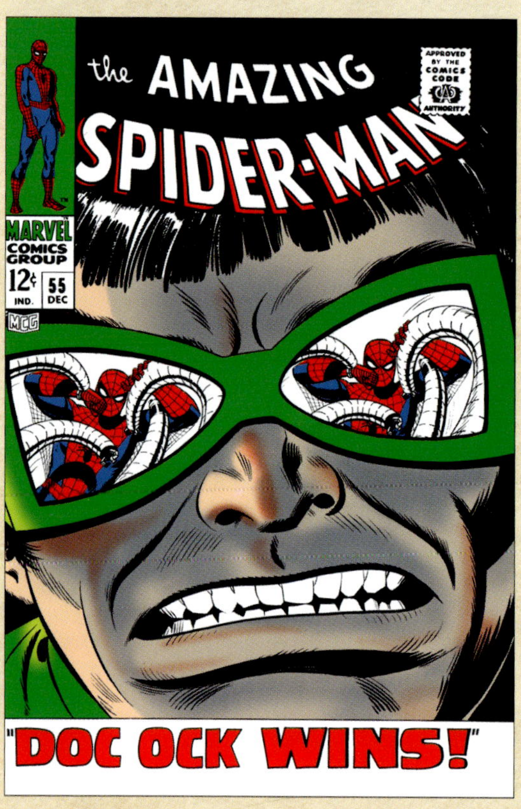
the AMAZING SPIDER-MAN
APPROVED BY THE COMICS CODE AUTHORITY
MARVEL COMICS GROUP
12¢ IND.
55 DEC
"DOC OCK WINS!"

SEPT
60¢ U.K. 25 P
#1
A MARVEL COMICS LIMITED SERIES
WOLVERINE

INTRODUCTION

As long as there have been stories, there have been heroes who appear larger than life. In ancient times there were Gilgamesh, Samson, and Hercules. Starting in the late 1930s the epic hero took on a new guise: the American Super Hero. Ever since then Marvel Comics has been most responsible for redefining and revolutionizing the Super Hero concept for successive generations of readers.

The heroes featured in this book are four of Marvel's most famous. Each reflects a different facet of the Super Hero concept as it has developed and changed through Marvel's long history.

The first of these four heroes to appear was Captain America. Co-created by Joe Simon and Jack Kirby on the eve of America's entry into World War II, Captain America embodied the noblest aspects of his nation. Dedicated to liberty and equality, Captain America has risked his life time and again to stop would-be tyrants from oppressing the innocent, both here and abroad. Captain America is brave, idealistic despite the evils he sees around him, and incorruptible. He represents the Super Hero concept at its purest.

Twenty-one years later, America's vision of itself had changed considerably. This was the cold war era, when America had become a "superpower" and people feared that a war with the Soviet Union would destroy all life on Earth. It was then that Stan Lee and Jack Kirby created Dr. Bruce Banner, the mild-mannered nuclear scientist who became a rampaging monster, the Hulk. If Captain America is the American flag in human form, then the Hulk is the H-bomb come to life, the disturbing underside of the American Super Hero myth. All the Hulk wants is to be left in peace, but to provoke his radiation-fueled rage is to invite one's destruction.

Later that same year, Stan Lee and Steve Ditko created a very different kind of Super Hero than those of the past. This newcomer was neither a confident icon of perfection like Captain America nor a bestial engine of destruction like the Hulk. Peter Parker was a teenager who gained his superhuman powers by sheer accident. From that time forward, by trial and error, Peter, as Spider-Man, has sought to use his unusual talents to make this world a better place. Super-powered he may be, but Spider-Man is an everyman whose struggles through life are essentially the same as our own.

A dozen years after Spider-Man's debut came that of the most recent of this Super Hero quartet, Wolverine of the mutant X-Men, whose identity combines aspects of his three predecessors. He longs to be a perfect hero like Captain America, but knows he cannot—like Bruce Banner, Wolverine has a monstrous side to his psyche that he will never escape. While the young Peter Parker struggles with his feelings of guilt and alienation, the older, wiser Wolverine grapples with his violent inner demons. Thus he too has become a hero for our complex times.

Together these four characters demonstrate the evolution of the Super Hero myth over more than sixty years. Each is very much a product of a particular period in American culture, yet each hero also remains vital and popular today. At the core of every great, enduring epic hero is something timeless. Each of these four legendary characters embodies unchanging aspects of humanity, and their stories continue to intrigue, inspire, and define the Super Hero concept.

CAPTAIN AMERICA
APRIL
10¢
No. 2
COMICS
UNITED STATES
45 SMASH PAGES of CAPTAIN AMERICA PLUS OTHER FEATURES
"TRAPPED in the NAZI STRONGHOLD!" Story on Page 17

CAPTAIN AMERICA

THE TIMELESS PERSONIFICATION OF EVERY AMERICAN'S HEROIC POTENTIAL

It was December 1940, and the Second World War had consumed Europe for nearly two years. Yet so far the United States remained at peace. Though today the Allies' struggle against Nazi Germany and the Axis powers is universally regarded as a just war, back then American opinion was sharply divided. President Franklin Roosevelt sought to aid the United Kingdom in its desperate struggle to fend off German attacks, but many Americans were isolationists, opposed to becoming involved in foreign conflicts. How surprising it must have been when readers saw the first issue of Captain America Comics. There on the cover was a Super Hero dressed like an American flag, punching Adolf Hitler in the jaw!

Thus, from the very beginning, "Captain America" incarnated America's democratic ideals and passion for freedom. He represented the side of his country that would not stand by and allow the forces of tyranny to prevail. Rather, Captain America embodied America's fighting spirit on behalf of liberty. A year later, after Japan attacked Pearl Harbor on December 7, the rest of America would join Captain America in his battle.

Debuting only three years after the first Super Hero—Superman—first appeared, Captain America was not the first costumed, patriotic-themed hero, but he was and remains the greatest. Captain America is also the most important creation from the team of writer Joe Simon and the late artist Jack Kirby. At the time, they worked for Timely Comics, which had entered the Super Hero genre in 1939 with the premier of the "Human Torch" and "Prince Namor the Sub-Mariner" in *Marvel Comics* #1. Timely would eventually become known as Marvel Comics in the 1960s.

The reason Captain America has proved such a powerful, enduring creation may lie in the brilliance of his origin. Simon and Kirby first told the saga in *Captain America Comics* #1, and subsequent writers elaborated on it. Their hero was Steve Rogers, a youth driven by his fervor to do whatever he could to stop the march of

AFTER HITTING NEWSSTANDS IN 1940 WITH A BLOW TO HITLER'S JAW, CAPTAIN AMERICA FOILED NAZI PLANS AGAIN IN ISSUE #2 AND CONTINUED TO CAPTURE THE AMERICAN FIGHTING SPIRIT THROUGHOUT THE SECOND WORLD WAR.

fascism abroad. Rogers tried desperately to join the army, but he was thin, frail, and sickly, and could not pass the physical. But a military officer was impressed by Rogers's passion to serve his country and offered him the opportunity to volunteer for a top-secret experiment.

President Roosevelt himself had authorized this project to create "super-soldiers," in imitation of Super Heroes like the Human Torch, to defend the nation against enemy agents. The project was titled "Operation Rebirth."

So young Rogers was brought to the secret laboratory of a scientific genius called "Professor Reinstein." This was Simon and Kirby's obvious allusion to Albert Einstein, and later stories asserted that "Reinstein" was the code name used by Dr. Abraham Erskine. "Reinstein" concocted a "super-soldier serum" that was administered to young Rogers. He then bombarded Rogers with "vita-rays."

The result was miraculous: the weak Steve Rogers rapidly grew healthier, more muscular, and even taller and smarter, until he had metamorphosed into a physically perfect specimen of humanity.

But one of the enemy agents Roosevelt sought to stop had succeeded in infiltrating Operation Rebirth. On witnessing Erskine's triumph, this spy, Heinz Kruger, shot him dead. The transformed Steve Rogers immediately

BELOW: IN *CAPTAIN AMERICA COMICS* #1, PRESIDENT ROOSEVELT SUGGESTED SARCASTICALLY THAT A SUPER HERO LIKE THE HUMAN TORCH MIGHT BE ABLE TO RID THE ARMY OF ITS SPY PROBLEM.

OPPOSITE: PROFESSOR REINSTEIN'S SUPER-SOLDIER SERUM GAVE PUNY STEVE ROGERS PHYSICAL STRENGTH TO MATCH HIS PATRIOTIC SPIRIT.

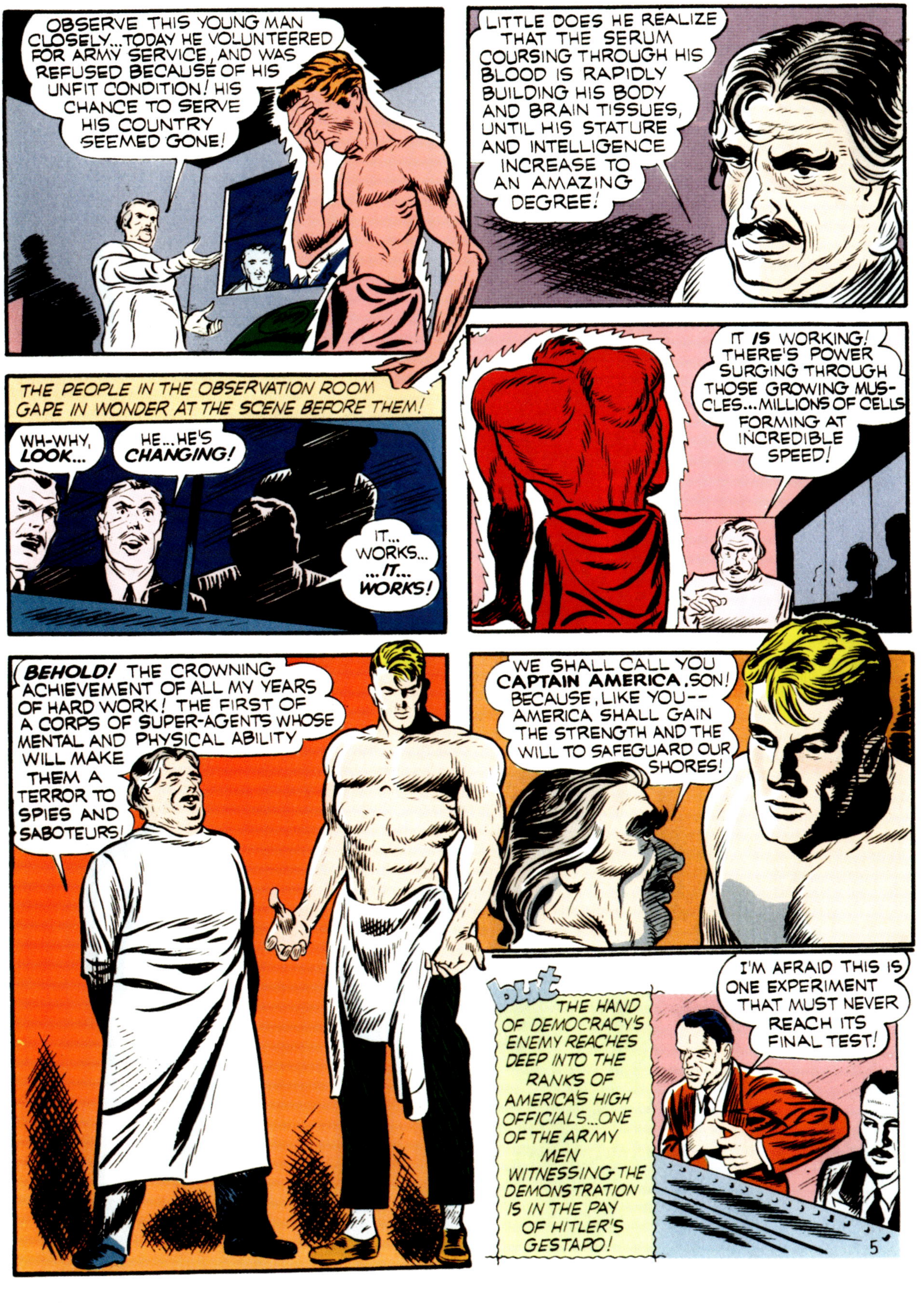
OBSERVE THIS YOUNG MAN CLOSELY...TODAY HE VOLUNTEERED FOR ARMY SERVICE, AND WAS REFUSED BECAUSE OF HIS UNFIT CONDITION! HIS CHANCE TO SERVE HIS COUNTRY SEEMED GONE!
LITTLE DOES HE REALIZE THAT THE SERUM COURSING THROUGH HIS BLOOD IS RAPIDLY BUILDING HIS BODY AND BRAIN TISSUES, UNTIL HIS STATURE AND INTELLIGENCE INCREASE TO AN AMAZING DEGREE!
THE PEOPLE IN THE OBSERVATION ROOM GAPE IN WONDER AT THE SCENE BEFORE THEM!
WH-WHY, LOOK...
HE...HE'S CHANGING!
IT... WORKS... ...IT... WORKS!
IT IS WORKING! THERE'S POWER SURGING THROUGH THOSE GROWING MUSCLES...MILLIONS OF CELLS FORMING AT INCREDIBLE SPEED!
BEHOLD! THE CROWNING ACHIEVEMENT OF ALL MY YEARS OF HARD WORK! THE FIRST OF A CORPS OF SUPER-AGENTS WHOSE MENTAL AND PHYSICAL ABILITY WILL MAKE THEM A TERROR TO SPIES AND SABOTEURS!
WE SHALL CALL YOU CAPTAIN AMERICA, SON! BECAUSE, LIKE YOU-- AMERICA SHALL GAIN THE STRENGTH AND THE WILL TO SAFEGUARD OUR SHORES!
BUT THE HAND OF DEMOCRACY'S ENEMY REACHES DEEP INTO THE RANKS OF AMERICA'S HIGH OFFICIALS...ONE OF THE ARMY MEN WITNESSING THE DEMONSTRATION IS IN THE PAY OF HITLER'S GESTAPO!
I'M AFRAID THIS IS ONE EXPERIMENT THAT MUST NEVER REACH ITS FINAL TEST!
5

DEATH TO THE DOGS OF DEMOCRACY!
UGH!
PROFESSOR REINSTEIN! WHAT--
BAM!
THE SPY'S MUFFLED GUN SPEAKS AGAIN BEFORE THE GROUP CAN RECOVER FROM ITS SURPRISE--THE VIAL CONTAINING THE VALUABLE SERUM SHATTERS INTO A THOUSAND PIECES!
CRASH!
HIS TREACHERY DISCOVERED--THE SPY TURNS HIS FIRE ON THE INFURIATED GROUP IN THE OBSERVATION ROOM--
LOOK OUT, MISTER GROVER!
BANG!
SUDDENLY THE ENEMY AGENT'S EYES WIDEN IN HORROR AS A TERRIBLE VENGEANCE IN THE FORM OF CAPTAIN AMERICA LEAPS TOWARD HIM!
COME ON OUT, YOU SKUNK!
SOC!
WHAM!
6

struck at Kruger, knocking him into a machine that electrocuted the assassin. Steve Rogers had won his first victory over the enemies of freedom, but the secret of the "super-soldier serum" had apparently died with Erskine. Steve Rogers would be America's only super-soldier.

The government wanted their super-soldier to become a symbol of America, and so it created the identity of "Captain America" for him. He wore the colors of the American flag, and his uniform even had stars and stripes.

In real life, writer Joe Simon claims to have drawn the first sketch of the Captain in costume. Jack Kirby told comics artist/historian Jim Steranko that they "gave him a chain mail shirt and a shield, like a modern-day crusader. The wings on his helmet were from Mercury, the god of speed. He symbolized the American dream."

Captain America originally carried a triangular shield, which also had stars and stripes. But soon Simon and Kirby gave him the familiar circular shield that he carries today. The Captain not only uses his shield for defense but also hurls it as a weapon. Moreover, in the 1960s it was established that the shield is virtually indestructible. Still later it would be explained that the shield is composed of an alloy of two fictional metals—the indestructible adamantium (the same steel alloy in Wolverine's skeleton) and vibranium (which absorbs vibrations)—and an unknown third component whose secret died with Erskine.

Captain America's original assignment was to combat spies and fifth columnists in the United States. The government gave him the cover identity of an army private stationed at Camp Lehigh. The Captain's writers derived considerable humor from Private Rogers's blustering superior, Sergeant Mike Duffy, who was wholly unaware of Rogers's double identity and considered him a hopeless incompetent.

Steve Rogers was an American everyman figure, and Captain America represented the heroic potential of any American loyal to his or her country and to its founding principles. As an army private, Rogers symbolized the heroism of the American fighting man. Every brave U.S. soldier was, in his own way, a Captain America. This has surely provided much of the character's appeal to generations of readers from the 1940s into the present day.

In the early decades of the Super Hero genre, heroes were often given kid sidekicks in the belief that children could more easily identify with characters closer to their own age. In Captain America's case, that sidekick was Bucky Barnes, Camp Lehigh's teenage "mascot." It would later be explained that the camp had adopted Bucky after his father had been killed in action.

OPPOSITE: CAPTAIN AMERICA GOT RIGHT TO WORK DISPATCHING NAZI SPIES. UNFORTUNATELY THE FIRST SECRET AGENT HE DISPOSED OF GOT TO PROFESSOR REINSTEIN FIRST.

ABOVE: HIS BATTLE AGAINST THE FIFTH COLUMN EARNED CAP AN INSTANT CELEBRITY, BOTH ON THE COMIC BOOK PAGES AND IN REAL-LIFE.

RIGHT AND OPPOSITE: BUCKY BARNES BECAME THE CAPTAIN'S SIDEKICK AND THE ENVY OF CHILDREN ALL OVER AMERICA BY ACCIDENTALLY DISCOVERING STEVE ROGERS'S SECRET IDENTITY.

BELOW: WITH MARVEL'S FIRST MAJOR SUPER HERO CAME ITS FIRST TERRIBLE VILLAIN, THE RED SKULL.

After Bucky accidentally discovered Rogers's dual identity, Rogers decided to make him Captain America's partner. Barnes wore a mask, though he was known in costume as "Bucky," which would seem to defeat the purpose of being disguised!

There was a third major character in the series; a figure who symbolized the opposite of everything Captain America—and the American Dream—represented. This was Captain America's eternal nemesis, the "Red Skull." One of comics' greatest villains, the Red Skull was to Hitler's Germany what Captain America was to America: the personification of their goals and ideals.

Moreover, while Captain America fought to save lives, the Red Skull embodied not only tyranny but also death itself. He wore a head mask in the form of a skull, colored blood red. In an early story the Skull established his calling card: after committing another murder, he whistled Chopin's "Funeral March."

The first version of the Red Skull debuted in a tale in *Captain America Comics* #1. At the end of the story, he was unmasked as industrialist George Maxon. But Maxon proved only to be impersonating the real Red Skull. Simon and Kirby had decided to keep their master villain's identity an enigma: over the many decades his true face has remained a mystery. The real Red Skull finally debuted in *Captain America Comics* #7, also whistling the "Funeral March."

Though created to embody the evil of Nazism, the Red Skull has proved relevant right into the twenty-first century. Even in the 1940s, the Red Skull's specialty was to spread fear among Germany's enemies by wreaking destruction. Although it was not then a widely used term, the Red Skull was what would today be called a terrorist.

Joe Simon and Jack Kirby made Captain America into one of Timely's star characters. Kirby was rapidly developing the dynamic art style that made him the most significant artist in the history of American comic books.

THAT SAME NIGHT... WHEN BUCKY VISITS STEVE'S TENT... HE MAKES A STARTLING DISCOVERY---
WHAT IN--?
HELLO... STEVE! I CAME DOWN TO-- WHA--WH--WHY YOU'RE CAPTAIN AMERICA!
YOU LITTLE RASCAL! I OUGHT TO TAN YOUR HIDE! I GUESS YOU GOT ME DEAD TO RIGHTS--- I AM CAPTAIN AMERICA!
GOSH... GEE WHIZ... GOLLY!! I... I NEVER THOUGHT...
FROM NOW ON WE MUST BOTH SHARE THIS SECRET TOGETHER... THAT MEANS YOU'RE MY PARTNER, BUCKY!
and... SO BUCKY'S DREAM IS FULFILLED AS HE FIGHTS SIDE BY SIDE WITH CAPTAIN AMERICA AGAINST THE VICIOUS ELEMENTS WHO SEEK TO OVERTHROW THE U.S. GOVERNMENT!
HERE IS HOW YOU CAN BECOME A MEMBER OF... CAPTAIN AMERICA'S SENTINELS OF LIBERTY and JOIN CAPTAIN AMERICA IN HIS WAR AGAINST THE SPIES AND ENEMIES IN OUR MIDST WHO THREATEN OUR VERY INDEPENDENCE....
SEND 10¢
to TIMELY PUBLICATIONS... 330 WEST 42ND ST. NEW YORK, N.Y. TO COVER COST OF MAILING... AND RECEIVE A REAL OFFICIAL BADGE AND MEMBERSHIP CARD!
CAPTAIN AMERICA
BUCKY
BETTY ROSS
SENTINEL OF LIBERTY No. 58
Member SENTINELS of LIBERTY
I SOLEMNLY PLEDGE TO UPHOLD THE PRINCIPLES OF THE SENTINELS OF LIBERTY AND ASSIST CAPTAIN AMERICA IN HIS WAR AGAINST SPIES IN THE U.S.A.
SIGNED___________
8

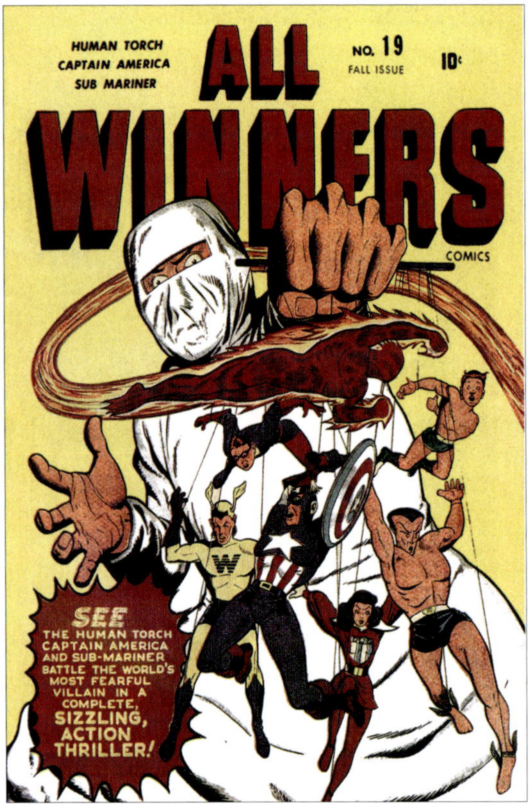

Issue #3 proved to be a landmark in comics history: it contained a text feature written by a teenage Timely staffer who would become the Super Hero genre's most innovative writer and editor in the 1960s: Stan Lee.

But Simon and Kirby did only ten issues of Captain America Comics before they left Timely for National Periodical Publications, now known as DC Comics. Even after Simon and Kirby's departure, Captain America's sales continued to rise under other writers such as Otto Binder, Bill Finger, and Stan Lee, and artists such as Al Avison, and the great cover artist Alex Schomburg. There was even a Captain America movie serial from Republic Pictures in 1943, testifying to the character's immense popularity.

The 1940s are now known as the "Golden Age of Comics," their first great period of popularity. In 1946, Timely first teamed Captain America up with the Human Torch, Sub-Mariner, and other Super Heroes as the "All Winners Squad" (in *All Winners Comics* #19), the forerunner of Marvel's Super Hero teams of the 1960s.

But after the end of World War II comics sales began to decline. Created to battle fascism, Captain America now found himself just another costumed crime fighter. It seemed that America's love affair with Super Heroes might have been merely a fad. Timely stopped publishing Captain America stories in 1949; by 1951, virtually all Super Heroes had disappeared and the "Golden Age" was over.

Comics turned to other genres to survive. The company now known as Marvel tried reviving its leading Super Heroes, the Torch, Sub-Mariner, and Captain America, in *Young Men* #24 in 1953. This time the Captain battled not Nazis but Communists. But the revival came too early, and the experiment swiftly fizzled.

Then, in 1956, DC Comics editor Julius Schwartz successfully launched a modernized version of one of his company's Golden Age heroes, the "Flash." Thus began the great Super Hero revival now known as the "Silver Age of Comics." It was in response to the success of Schwartz's Justice League comics that Marvel writer/ editor Stan Lee and artist Jack Kirby, who had returned to Marvel near the end of 1958, co-created Marvel's

OPPOSITE: (LEFT) CAP TEAMED UP WITH THE HUMAN TORCH AND SUB-MARINER TO FORM THE FIRST OF MANY MARVEL SUPER HERO TEAMS, THE ALL WINNERS SQUAD. (RIGHT) *STRANGE TALES* #114 REMINDED READERS OF THE BELOVED WORLD WAR II-ERA SUPER HERO.

LEFT: CAP MADE HIS TRIUMPHANT RETURN IN THE *AVENGERS* #4.

first Silver Age heroes, the "Fantastic Four," in 1961. Among them was a new, modern version of the Human Torch. Then, in *Fantastic Four* #4 in 1962, Lee and Kirby brought back the original Sub-Mariner.

It now seemed inevitable that Timely's third great star, Captain America, would return as well. Lee proclaimed on the cover of *Strange Tales* #114 (November 1963): "Captain America returns to challenge the Human Torch!" But this wasn't the real Captain: instead Lee and Kirby had the new Torch's enemy, the Acrobat, disguise himself as Captain America. Perhaps Lee and Kirby were attempting to test reader reactions to the idea of reviving Captain America.

Just as the Sub-Mariner had returned in *Fantastic Four* #4, so too did Lee and Kirby bring back the real Captain America in the fourth issue of another new Super Hero team series, the Avengers (March 1964). In the Arctic, Namor, who had resurfaced as an enemy of the "Avengers," came across natives worshipping the figure of a blond-haired man entombed in a block of ice. Characteristically flying into a rage at what he considered idol worship, the Sub-Mariner hurled the block of ice into the sea, where it floated south, slowly melting as the water grew warmer. The blond man, who wore an American soldier's uniform, was found by the Avengers, who were in a submarine, tracking Namor down. The Avengers saw that the man wore Captain America's costume beneath the tatters of his military garb and also had Captain America's shield strapped to his body. They were astonished, since Captain America had disappeared towards the end of World War II. (Lee and Kirby had chosen to ignore the postwar Captain America stories.) Abruptly Captain America woke, shouting for Bucky.

The Avengers calmed the distraught hero, who then revealed to them what had happened to him in the war's final days. Captain America and Bucky had tried to stop their Nazi enemy, "Baron Zemo," from stealing an experimental drone plane being developed by the Allies. Zemo launched the plane toward Germany, and the Captain and Bucky, dressed as soldiers, sped after it on a motorcycle and leaped aboard in an attempt to stop it. But the plane had been booby-trapped and exploded, killing

BELOW AND OPPOSITE: THE AVENGERS WERE SHOCKED TO DISCOVER CAPTAIN AMERICA WAS STILL ALIVE AND TO HEAR WHAT HAD HAPPENED TO HIM AND BUCKY IN THE FINAL DAYS OF THE WAR.

Bucky and dropping Captain America into the icy waters of the North Atlantic. There Captain America went into suspended animation, so he had not aged in the years since the war. Later writers would explain that it was the super-soldier serum that caused him to go into suspended animation instead of drowning.

Why kill off Bucky? Stan Lee has explained in interviews that he simply never liked the character. One way that Lee and his collaborators at Marvel revolutionized Super Hero comics in the 1960s was by depicting their personalities more realistically. Presumably Lee and Kirby found the concept of the costumed kid sidekick dated.

Notice that Lee and Kirby did not choose to create an entirely new version of Captain America, as they had with the Human Torch, who was reinvented as a teenager for the Fantastic Four—a role completely unrelated to any of the previous Human Torch stories. It was essential to their treatment of Captain America that he was indeed Steve Rogers. Like Rip Van Winkle, Captain America had slept for decades and woken to find a world vastly changed from the one he knew. He felt out of place. Captain America embodied the fervent, idealistic patriotism of World War II America, suddenly thrust into the social and political upheavals of the 1960s.

Moreover, the Captain was now haunted by guilt. Bucky was like a son to him, and Rogers blamed himself for failing to prevent Bucky's death.

The original lineup of the Avengers included several of Marvel's leading heroes of the early 1960s: "Thor," "Iron Man," "Giant-Man," and the "Wasp." They enthusiastically inducted Captain America into their team, and the American public, as depicted in *Avengers* #1, hailed the return of this long lost hero.

Hiding in a South American jungle, Baron Heinrich Zemo also learned that the man he thought he had killed two decades before had turned up alive. Zemo vowed to finish the task once and for all.

Zemo was not a villain from the Golden Age, but a new creation of Lee and Kirby. Working secretly as one of the Third Reich's leading scientists, Zemo wore a mask to conceal his identity. He created "Adhesive

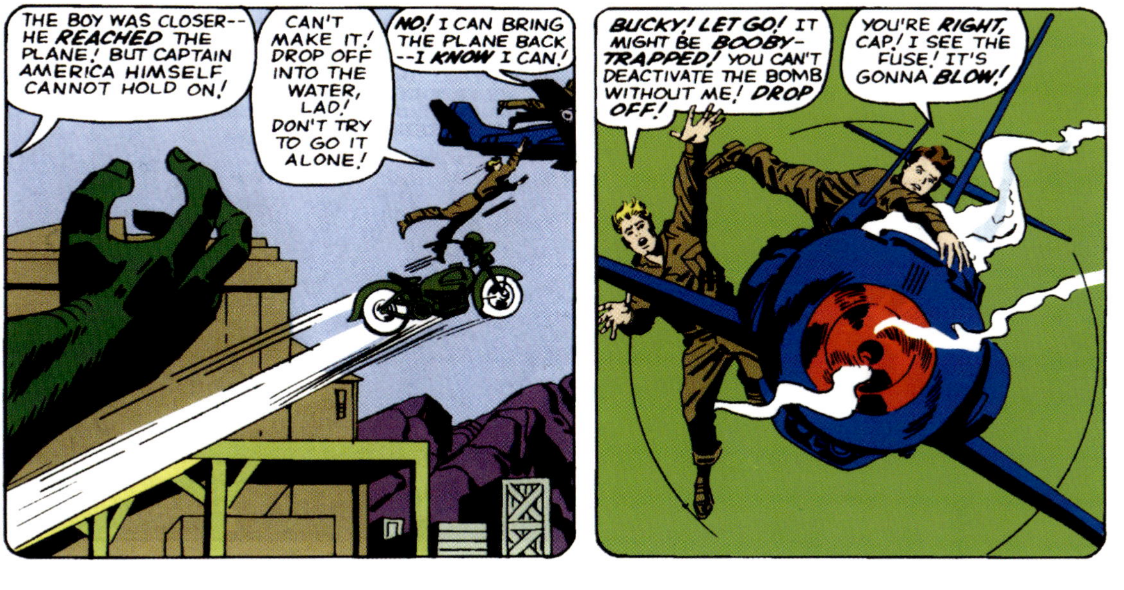

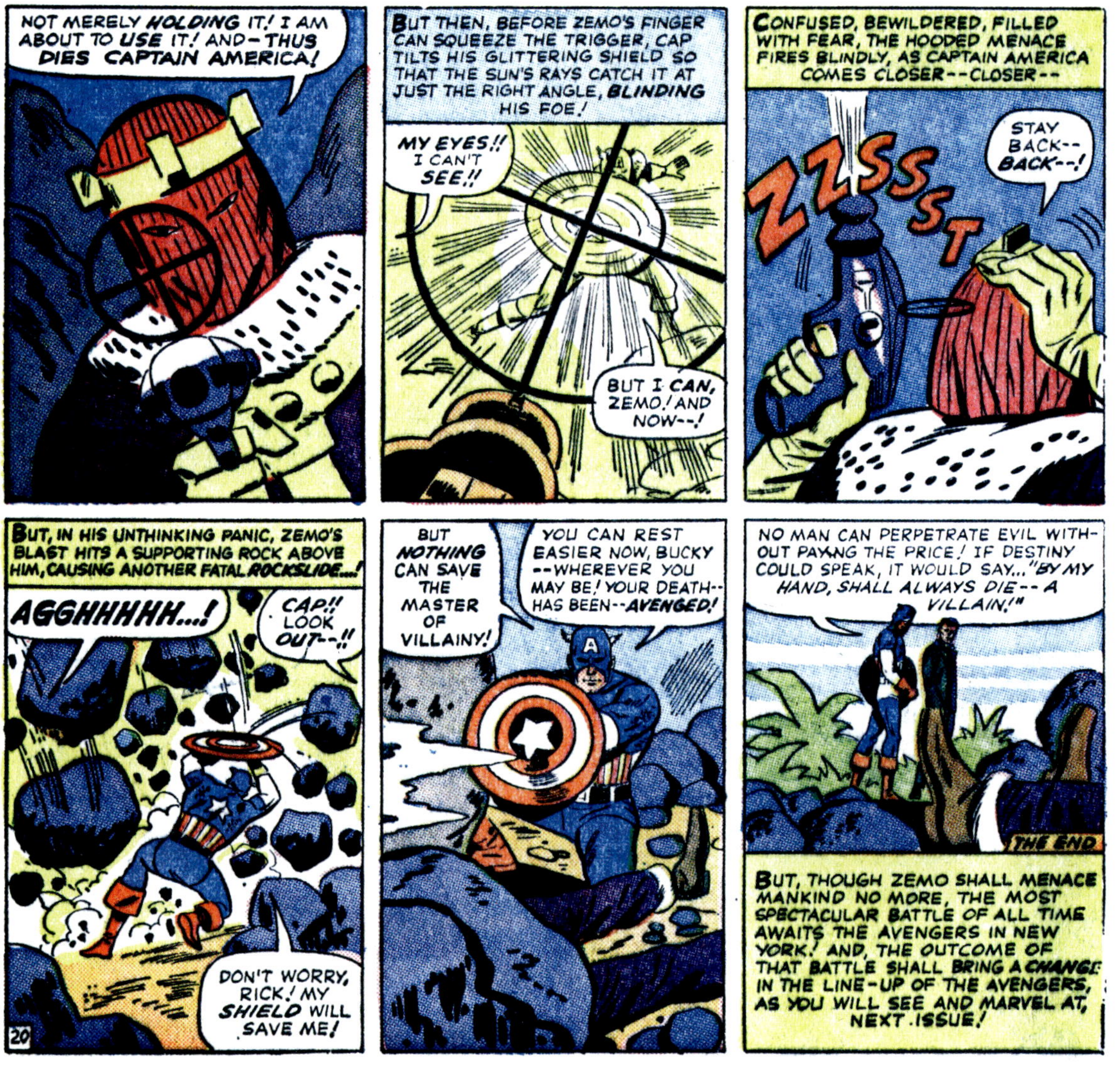

X," a form of paste that permanently adhered to any surface. In trying to stop Zemo during the war, it was explained, Captain America had hurled his shield at a tank of Adhesive X, inadvertently causing it to splash over Zemo, permanently affixing his mask to his head. (How Zemo managed to eat after that, Lee and Kirby never explained.)

Zemo formed a team of super-villains called the Masters of Evil, who clashed repeatedly with the Avengers. Finally, in *Avengers* #15 (April 1965), Captain America tracked Zemo to his South American stronghold. Zemo aimed a death-ray gun at his nemesis, who tilted his shield to reflect intense sunlight into Zemo's eyes. Temporarily blinded, Zemo fired wildly, triggering an avalanche in which he was killed. Captain America had finally avenged Bucky's death.

Before this, Lee and Kirby had inaugurated a new Captain America series in another Marvel title, Tales of Suspense, starting with the November 1964 issue. Tales was a "split book": Iron Man took up the first half of each comic, and Captain America filled the second half. The first several installments were set in the present, but with issue #63 (March 1965), Lee and Kirby shifted the series back to the 1940s, perhaps in part to avoid conflicts with Avengers continuity. Some of these stories were retellings of the original Simon and Kirby Captain America tales from the 1940s, including issue #63's retelling of the origin story. Another was a remake of the first Red Skull story from 1941, thereby introducing Captain America's archenemy to a new generation of readers.

With issue #66 (June 1965) Lee and Kirby began doing new stories set during World War II. Whereas Simon and Kirby had kept Private Steve Rogers on the home front, Lee and Kirby now showed Captain America and Bucky fighting in Europe.

The first new wartime story was "The Fantastic Origin of the Red Skull," a sinister parallel to the Captain's own origin tale. The Skull was originally an impoverished German drifter. Lee and Kirby did not reveal his real name, but a later writer, J. M. DeMatteis, gave him the most generic German name possible: "Johann Schmidt," or, in English translation, "John Smith." He was an everyman whose fate took an evil

OPPOSITE: A FATAL LANDSLIDE KILLED BARON ZEMO, AND BUCKY'S DEATH WAS AVENGED.

BELOW: (CLOCKWISE FROM BOTTOM RIGHT) AFTER CAP BEGAN STARRING OPPOSITE IRON MAN IN TALES OF SUSPENSE, STAN LEE AND JACK KIRBY INTRODUCED A CAPTAIN AMERICA SERIES SET IN WORLD WAR II TO AVOID CONFLICTS WITH HIS ROLE IN THE AVENGERS.

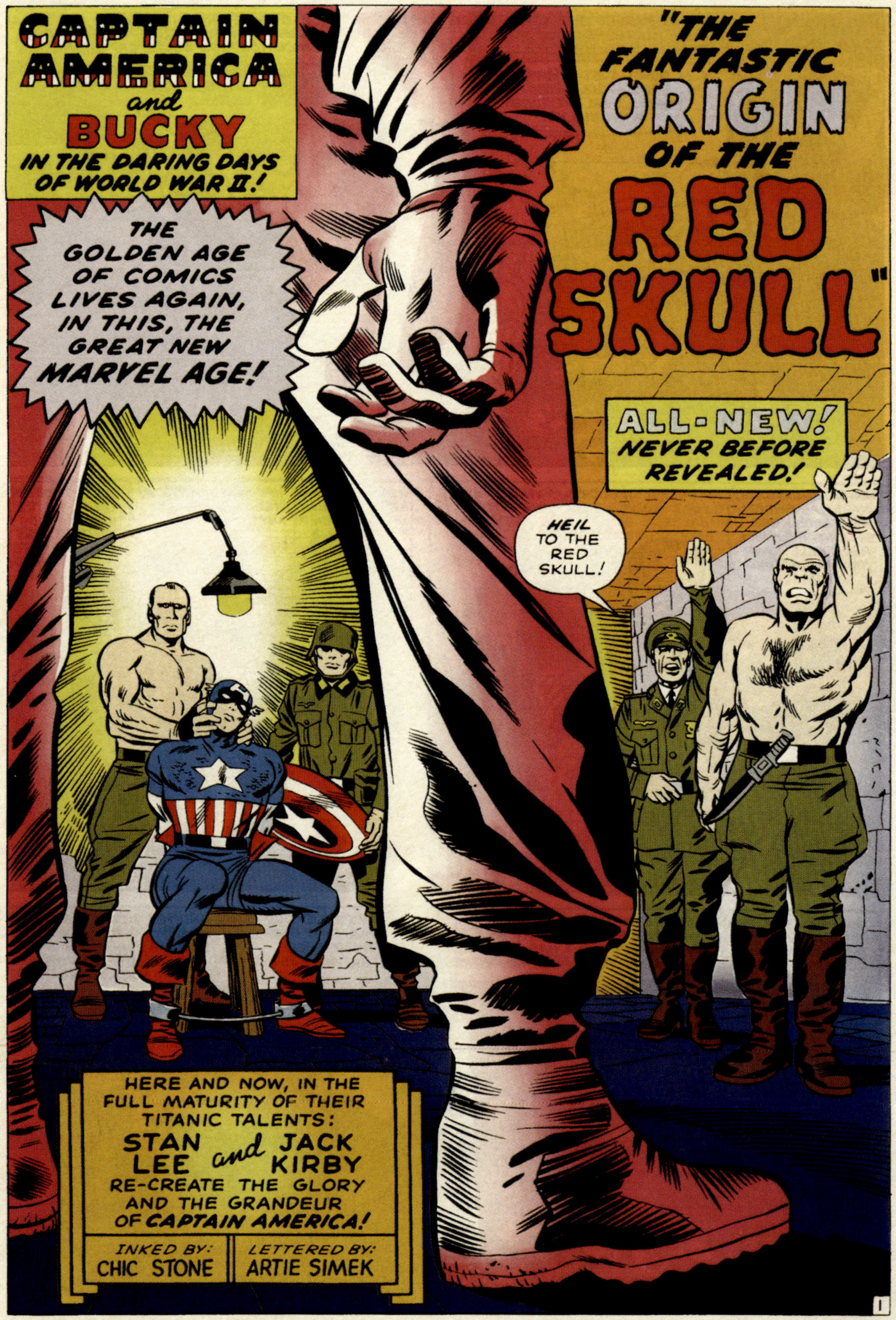

CAPTAIN AMERICA and BUCKY IN THE DARING DAYS OF WORLD WAR II!
"THE FANTASTIC ORIGIN OF THE RED SKULL"
THE GOLDEN AGE OF COMICS LIVES AGAIN, IN THIS, THE GREAT NEW MARVEL AGE!
ALL-NEW! NEVER BEFORE REVEALED!
HEIL TO THE RED SKULL!
HERE AND NOW, IN THE FULL MATURITY OF THEIR TITANIC TALENTS: STAN LEE and JACK KIRBY RE-CREATE THE GLORY AND THE GRANDEUR OF CAPTAIN AMERICA!
INKED BY: CHIC STONE
LETTERED BY: ARTIE SIMEK
1

turn. Embittered by life, the drifter was working as a lowly bellboy in a hotel when Adolf Hitler came to stay. Berating one of his subordinates, Hitler thundered that he could turn this bellboy into a better soldier than he was. Looking into the bellboy's eyes, Hitler was mesmerized, recognizing an intensity of hatred comparable to his own. Hitler himself trained the bellboy to become the Third Reich's most dangerous terrorist, and created for him the masked identity of the Red Skull to inspire fear in Germany's enemies. Hitler succeeded only too well, and Lee had Hitler confess that even he came to fear the power of the Red Skull.

Over in the Avengers, Captain America returned from South America in issue #16 (May 1965) to discover that the heroes who had inducted him into the team were now all leaving for various reasons. (In real life, Jack Kirby, who drew and co-plotted the series, was leaving the book.) Captain America stayed on with a team of new Avengers recruits, who were all newly reformed villains from other Marvel series: "Hawkeye," "Quicksilver," and the "Scarlet Witch." Whereas in the original Avengers, Captain America was one among equals, now he was the new Avengers' leader, keeping these rebellious recruits in line. Though physically little older than the others thanks to his stint in suspended animation, Captain America was far more experienced and became something of a father figure to the new Avengers. Longtime Marvel readers have fond memories of the days of "Cap's Kooky Quartet," as they were nicknamed, as written by Lee and drawn by Don Heck.

Continuing the tradition that Lee and Kirby inaugurated, the Avengers lineup has continually changed over the last forty years. At times Captain America has been the Avengers' chairman; other times he has not, and sometimes he takes long leaves of absence from active duty. Nonetheless, from the days of "Cap's Kooky Quartet" into the present, Captain America

OPPOSITE: THE OPENING PAGE OF *TALES OF SUSPENSE* #66.

BELOW: HITLER'S FATEFUL ENCOUNTER WITH THE BELLMAN WHO WOULD BECAME HIS "PERFECT NAZI."

has always been regarded as the leader of the team. If any hero can be said to be the heart of the Avengers, it is Captain America.

With issue #72 of *Tales of Suspense* (December 1965), Lee and Kirby made a smooth transition from Captain America's wartime exploits back into the present. They presented the final wartime battle between Captain America and the Red Skull, set in an underground bunker during the fall of Berlin. (So, oddly, Zemo must have tried to steal that drone plane after the Allies invaded Berlin!) Struck down by falling rubble, seemingly dying, the Red Skull defiantly told Captain America that three "Sleepers" would eventually avenge the Third Reich's defeat. Before the Skull could explain further, the bunker caved in, burying him. Then, in the present, Nazi agents activated three immense robots, the Sleepers, which together formed a doomsday machine that would have

BELOW: ON DEATH'S DOORSTEP, THE RED SKULL PROPHESIZED THE RESURRECTION OF THE THIRD REICH.

OPPOSITE: PEGGY CARTER, A LOVE INTEREST FROM CAP'S PAST, REEMERGED IN A FLASHBACK IN *TALES OF SUSPENSE* #75.

destroyed the planet had Captain America not found a way to stop them. Here and in other 1960s stories, this 1940s icon now found himself battling science-fiction menaces.

In issue #75 (March 1966) Lee and Kirby created a flashback that introduced Captain America's wartime girlfriend, an unnamed French Resistance fighter. In the present day in that same issue, the Captain encountered that woman's look-alike, "Agent 13" of "S.H.I.E.L.D.," the super-scientific spy organization Lee and Kirby had recently created in Strange Tales. Not surprisingly, Agent 13 became Captain America's new romantic interest for the 1960s and 1970s. Subsequent stories would reveal that her real name was Sharon Carter and that she was the younger sister of the aforementioned woman from Captain America's past, Peggy Carter, who proved to still be alive.

Tales of Suspense #75 also introduced one of the Captain's most memorable opponents, "Batroc the Leaper," a master of "la savate," the fighting method now better known as kickboxing. Through the dialogue he gave him, Lee turned the swaggering Batroc into an amusing stereotype of a Frenchman. Captain America tended to regard Batroc more as a nuisance than as an outright villain. Batroc has a sense of honor and has even allied himself with the Captain on occasion.

Lee and Kirby were clearly so fascinated by the Red Skull that they could not leave him dead in that Berlin bunker; "The Red Skull Lives" revealed the title of their story in *Tales of Suspense* #79 (July 1966). Luckily for him, he had been buried alive next to canisters of experimental gas that cast him into suspended animation—just as Captain America had been!

The Red Skull story arc in *Tales of Suspense* #79–81 is the peak of Lee and Kirby's Captain America series of the 1960s. The Skull, this comic-book embodiment of real-life Nazi evil, had also entered the world of Space Age science fiction. From "A.I.M.," an organization of criminal scientists, the Skull stole the Cosmic Cube, an object that could convert thoughts into reality. Holding the Cube, the Red Skull gained ultimate power; he created a suit of glittering armor for himself and prepared to make himself master of the planet. But the Skull could not give up his obsession with his old enemy Captain America. Revealing that it was he who ordered

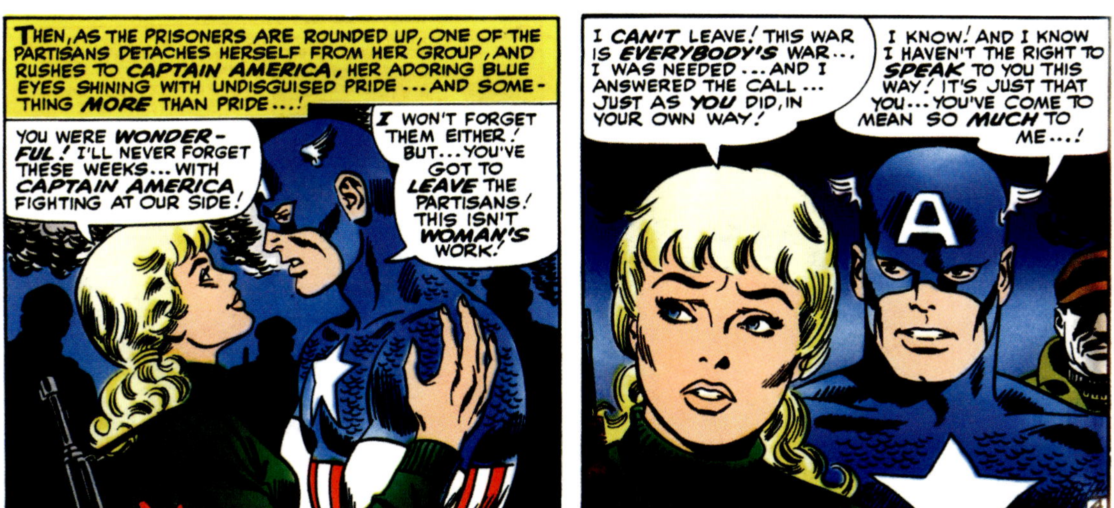

CAPTAIN AMERICA
AT LAST!! YOU ARE ABOUT TO MEET THE MOST INFAMOUS, MOST STARTLING, MOST FEARED VILLAIN OF THE GOLDEN AGE OF COMICS, AS HE LIVES AGAIN, IN THIS, THE MARVEL AGE...!
THE RED SKULL STRIKES!
WE TRIED AN EXPERIMENT IN THIS TALE! SINCE IT FEATURES A MENACE FROM THE PAST, WE WROTE IT IN THE STYLE OF THE 1940'S, BECAUSE SO MANY OF YOU HAVE WONDERED HOW THESE STORIES WERE WRITTEN YEARS AGO! WELL, NOW YOU'RE GONNA FIND OUT...!
By STAN LEE and JACK KIRBY
INKING: CHIC STONE
LETTERING: S.ROSEN

ETERNAL OPPOSITES

The team of writer Roger Stern and artist John Byrne established that the United States government created the costumed identity of Captain America for Steve Rogers to make him America's answer to Nazi Germany's mysterious terrorist, the Red Skull. Both men were symbols: one for a passionate will to fight for liberty and the other for the power of tyranny to spread fear and destruction.

Stern and Byrne were acknowledging what had become of these two characters in the decades since Joe Simon and Jack Kirby co-created them. Captain America and the Red Skull were polar opposites and natural archenemies. It was no wonder that both the Captain and the Red Skull (or, rather, one of his pawns impersonating him) both debuted in the first issue of *Captain America Comics* in 1941. They were linked from the start. They are in a sense inseparable. Freedom defines itself in relation to its opposite, which is tyranny. So too Captain America and the Red Skull are defined by their eternal opposition to each other.

If Captain America battles to save innocent people's lives from tyrants, then the Red Skull, befitting his name, is the agent of death. One of the Skull's trademarks is his "dust of death," which not only kills his victims but tightens and discolors the skin on their faces, until the corpses' heads resemble red skulls. Thus the Red Skull "signs" his murders.

Stan Lee played with the notion that the Red Skull is symbolically Captain America's "evil twin" in a story arc in which the Skull used the all-powerful Cosmic Cube to switch bodies with his nemesis (*Captain America* #115–119, July to November 1969).

Years later, the "evil twin" metaphor became a literal reality. Having decided that the Red Skull was a dated character, editor Mark Gruenwald had the effects of the suspended animation gas that had preserved the Skull's life wear off, leaving him an elderly man, who finally succumbed to death in *Captain America* #300 (December 1984). However, after becoming the Captain's writer, Gruenwald realized that the Skull was an essential part of the Captain America series. So Gruenwald resurrected the Skull by revealing that the Nazi genetic engineer had transferred the Skull's mind into a body cloned from that of Captain America himself. The Red Skull was now Captain America's literal double!

Like the Captain, the Red Skull is a man of the 1940s who slept for years to awake in a very different time. Though the Third Reich may be dead, through his modern stories the Skull demonstrates how the evils that founded Nazism take new forms in the present.

OPPOSITE: *TALES OF SUSPENSE* #65 RE-INTRODUCED THE RED SKULL TO CAPTAIN AMERICA'S "MARVEL AGE" FANS. RIGHT: "TITANIC TALENTS" STAN LEE AND JACK KIRBY CO-CREATED "THE ORIGIN OF THE RED SKULL" IN *SUSPENSE* #66, COMPLETE WITH NEW, MORE TYRANNICAL DIALOGUE FROM LEE.

RIGHT: WITH THE COSMIC CUBE IN HIS POSSESSION THE RED SKULL WAS FREE TO RULE ALL MANKIND.

OPPOSITE: FINALLY CAP HAD HIS OWN BOOK AGAIN WHEN *TALES OF SUSPENSE* #100 WAS RELEASED WITH A NEW NAME: *CAPTAIN AMERICA*.

Zemo to kill Bucky, the Red Skull turned the power of the Cosmic Cube against Captain America, but toyed with him, like a cat with a mouse, giving the Captain the opportunity to turn the tables. In grappling with his nemesis, the Red Skull dropped the Cube, a cataclysm destroyed the island on which he and the Captain were fighting, and the Skull was swallowed up by the waves.

It seemed that the Red Skull was at last dead, but the key word here is "seemed." Ever since then, the Red Skull has repeatedly returned from apparent death to menace Captain America and the world time and again. Though Hitler and his Third Reich are long gone, the Red Skull remains one of comics' greatest figures of evil. Just as Captain America represents the enduring spirit of American ideals and liberties, so too the Red Skull has come to embody the evil of totalitarianism as it takes new forms in new decades.

Marvel's innovative approach to the Super Hero genre in the 1960s brought the company amazing success. Iron Man was spun off into his own monthly comic book, and with issue #100 (April 1968) *Tales of Suspense* was retitled *Captain America*, who now had the whole book to himself.

Jack Kirby drew and co-plotted the first ten issues, but Stan Lee then collaborated with the brilliant young writer/artist Jim Steranko, acclaimed for his cinematic approach to comics. In this story arc, Rick Jones, the teenage confidant of the Hulk, became Captain America's new sidekick, wearing Bucky's costume. But Lee apparently lost interest in Rick's new role after Steranko's stint was over.

Instead, Lee found Captain America a very different kind of partner. Another of Marvel's great Silver Age artists, Gene Colan, came aboard the series, and in issue #117 (September 1969) he and Lee co-created a new costumed ally for the Captain: Sam Wilson, alias the "Falcon," who had what proved to be a telepathic bond with his pet falcon, "Redwing." What made the Falcon a revolutionary character was that he was African American. Several years earlier Lee and Kirby had created the first black hero in mainstream comics, the "Black Panther," in Fantastic Four. The Falcon was the first African-American Super Hero from a major comics company to take a prominent role.

CAP, IN HIS OWN MAGAZINE AT LAST!
APPROVED BY THE COMICS CODE AUTHORITY
CAPTAIN AMERICA
MARVEL COMICS GROUP
12¢ IND.
100 APR
MCG
BIG PREMIERE ISSUE!

RIGHT: THE FALCON, THE FIRST AFRICAN-AMERICAN SUPER HERO PRODUCED BY A MAINSTREAM COMICS COMPANY, PREMIERED IN *CAPTAIN AMERICA* #117.

OPPOSITE: (TOP) IN AN HOMAGE TO *EASY RIDER*, CAP HIT THE ROAD ON A MOTORCYCLE IN THE LATE 1960S; (BOTTOM) EVEN THE FALCON COULD NOT TELL THE FAKE CAP FROM THE REAL CAP.

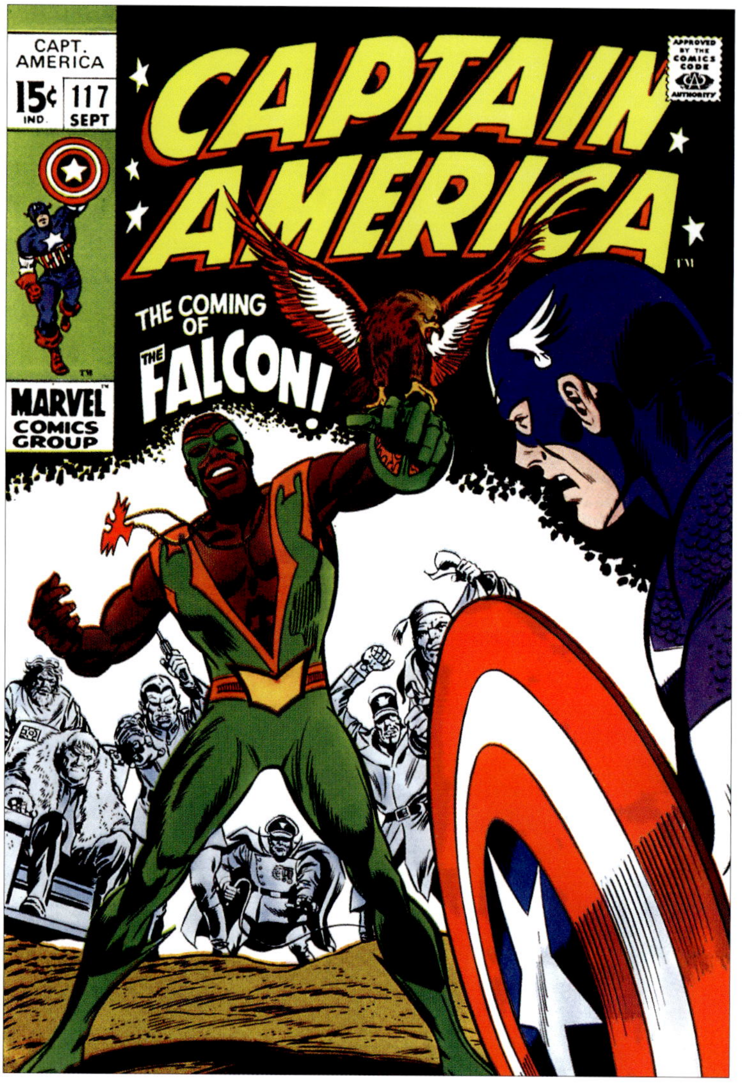

One of the landmark movies of the late 1960s was *Easy Rider*, in which Peter Fonda portrayed a biker who called himself "Captain America." In apparent acknowledgement, Stan Lee sent the real Captain America traveling the country on a motorcycle in the comics.

Soon, however, Lee returned Captain America to New York City as his home base and had Steve Rogers get a job as another of America's uniformed protectors: the World War II soldier was now a New York City policeman. More importantly, Lee teamed the Captain up with the Falcon and, with issue #134 (February 1971), even retitled the comic Captain America and the Falcon.

This is yet another example of how the Captain America series has remained relevant over the decades by addressing social and political issues of the time. Lee and Kirby had pioneered the use of positive black characters in mainstream comics. In partnering Captain America and the Falcon, Lee acknowledged the way America had changed in the wake of the civil rights movement of the 1960s.

In the early 1970s, Stan Lee wound down his writing work in order to concentrate on his growing responsibilities as a Marvel executive. Issue #141 (September 1971) was Lee's last as writer of Captain America; he was succeeded first by Gary Friedrich and then by Gerry Conway.

But the next major phase of Captain America's history was written by Steve Englehart. In an effort to make Captain America fit better into a Marvel Universe full of super-powered characters, Englehart endowed him with super-strength in issue #158, but this experiment did not last long.

More significantly, in issues #153–156 (September to December 1972), Englehart fit the 1950s "Captain America" stories from Young Men into the new continuity, in which the "real" Captain was said to have vanished in 1945. The 1950s Captain America was revealed to be a scholar who had rediscovered the super-soldier serum and used it to give him and a Bucky-look-alike sidekick superhuman strength. The unnamed scholar underwent plastic surgery to resemble Steve Rogers—he even adopted Rogers's name—and offered his services as Captain

America to the U.S. government. But the new Cap and Bucky had not been irradiated by "vita-rays" as Rogers had been, and as a result they grew paranoid about the "Red menace" and turned increasingly violent. Eventually, the government placed the 1950s Captain and Bucky in suspended animation. A disgruntled right-winger revived these two fanatics in the 1970s, so the real Captain had to stop them.

Englehart dealt openly with political themes in his Captain America run, and here he was attacking the Cold War paranoia that was so evident in the 1950s stories. He also dealt with a more contemporary concern, corporate crime, through the introduction of the corrupt multinational corporation, "Roxxon Oil."

In Englehart's most startling story arc, a political organization called the "Committee to Regain America's Principles" framed Captain America for murder and then smeared his reputation through the news media. The Committee proved to be a front for the "Secret Empire," a conspiracy against—and within—the federal government. Captain America finally pursued the leader of the Secret Empire into the Oval Office of the White House. Readers did not see the leader's unmasked face, but Captain America did and was horrified. Was it the president himself?

OPPOSITE AND BELOW: CAP FOUGHT AND DEFEATED THE SCHOLAR WHO HAD STOLEN HIS IDENTITY IN THE 1950S.

Englehart had devised a parallel to the Watergate scandal of the mid-1970s and its effect on the way so many Americans perceived their government. Utterly disillusioned, Steve Rogers abandoned his Captain America identity, eventually taking on the new costumed persona of "Nomad," the man without a country.

Eventually the Red Skull resurfaced once more and brutally murdered a boy who had attempted to become the new Captain America. This shocked Rogers into realizing he could not abandon his responsibilities, and he became Captain America anew. But from then on, the Captain would no longer accept government authority without question. He would follow his own conscience; government policy might diverge from American ideals, but Captain America never would. Other writers would follow in Englehart's path, pitting the government establishment against this dedicated American idealist.

At this time writer/editor Roy Thomas harked back to bygone days when the difference between right and wrong seemed clearer. In 1975 Thomas and artist Frank Robbins launched The Invaders, a new series set during World War II that teamed Captain America and Bucky up with the Sub-Mariner and the original Human Torch. The premise was that following the attack on Pearl Harbor, British Prime Minister Winston Churchill had asked these heroes to band together to "invade" occupied Europe and battle the Nazis there.

In time for the nation's bicentennial, Jack Kirby returned to the character he helped create, this time both writing and drawing Captain America and the Falcon. Kirby's wild and fertile imagination produced such characters as the "Royalists," conspirators in powdered wigs and eighteenth-century costumes, who planned to turn America into a monarchy. Prophetically, Kirby co-created a new ally for the Red Skull: Arnim Zola, who was what would now be called a genetic engineer. Kirby even revealed that Rogers's own ancestor had been a costumed hero in the Revolutionary War.

For an all-too-brief period in the early 1980s, the team of writer Roger Stern and John Byrne, one of the leading comics artists of his generation, collaborated on a superb run of Captain America issues. Reemphasizing that Steve Rogers was a man removed from his own time, they co-created a new girlfriend for him: Bernadette Rosenthal, a bohemian artist who was very much a child of the 1960s. In Stern and Byrne's most memorable story, Captain America was invited to run for president. In the end the Captain declined, believing it was more important for him to try to live as a symbol of American ideals, without the compromises of political realities.

Unless Captain America's writers take pains to address contemporary issues in their stories, this Golden Age hero runs the risk of seeming dated. Indeed, his series was in danger of cancellation when the late Mark Gruenwald took over as writer, infusing the book with so many new concepts that he kept the continuity going successfully for ten years. Gruenwald devised new adversaries who reflected changing times, such as "Flag-Smasher," a terrorist leader who was opposed to the very concept of nationhood. Steve Englehart had invented the Red Skull's "dust of death," which made his victims' heads look like red skulls. Gruenwald and artist Kieron Dwyer subjected the Skull to his own medicine: now the "red skull" was not a mask but the villain's real face. Gruenwald also tested the Captain's ideals by giving him a new romantic interest: the female costumed criminal "Diamondback."

RIGHT: IN "THE TRUTH," CAPTAIN AMERICA LEARNED THAT THE SUPER-SOLDIER SERUM WAS TESTED ON AFRICAN-AMERICAN SOLDIERS.

OPPOSITE: FROM MARVEL'S 9/11 BENEFIT BOOK, *HEROES*.

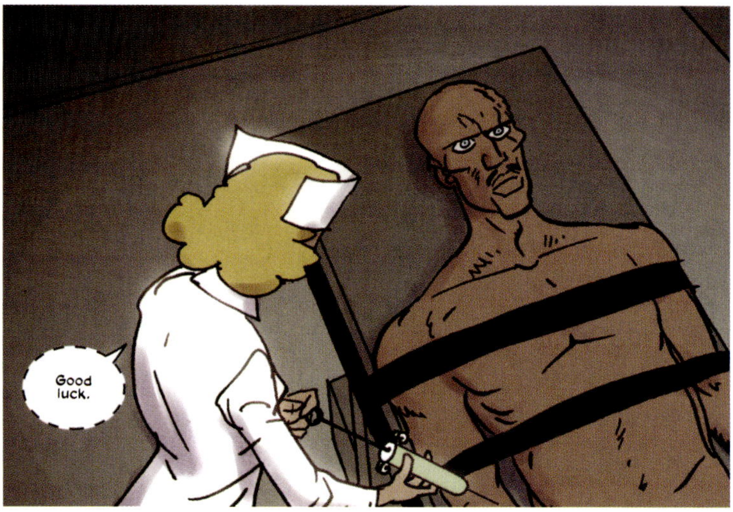

In his own most important story arc, Gruenwald worked a variation on Englehart's. When a government commission insisted that he obey their orders, Steve Rogers quit as Captain America rather than violate his conscience. Once again, Rogers eventually adopted a new costumed identity, calling himself simply the "Captain." But this time the government appointed a rival patriotic hero, the "Super-Patriot," to become the new Captain America. Lacking Rogers's strong moral code, the Super-Patriot turned into a brutal enforcer, inadvertently proving that the costume did not make the man. Ultimately Rogers reclaimed his identity as Captain America by defeating his successor, and the commission agreed to allow the real Captain to follow his own conscience as before.

Over the last dozen years or so, a succession of new writers have repeatedly shaken up the status quo in Captain America's adventures, in the never-ending effort to keep this legendary character relevant to new generations of readers. Writer Mark Waid and artist Ron Garney crafted yet another variation on a recurring theme of Captain America versus his own government. Framed once more as a criminal, Steve Rogers was deprived of his citizenship, literally becoming for a time a "Man without a Country," until the truth was revealed. Writer John Ney Rieber pitted Captain America against terrorists in his "New Deal" story line, confronting the Captain with accusations of American wrongdoing abroad. Perhaps the most shocking recent story line was "The Truth," written by Robert Morales and illustrated by Kyle Baker. In it, Captain America faces the "truth" about American racism when he discovers that African-American soldiers were forced to serve as test subjects for early versions of the super-soldier serum with horrifying results.

These kinds of stories are what have kept Captain America vital into the twenty-first century. From the very beginning, the Captain America series has asked what it means to be an American. Captain America is the adversary of all enemies of freedom, whether they are from outside the United States—the Nazis, the Soviets, the stateless terrorists—or are Americans acting in violation of their nation's laws and traditions.

In the aftermath of the September 11 attacks, the image of Captain America, comics' foremost icon of patriotism, took on renewed relevance. Perhaps the most striking image in Marvel's 9/11 benefit book, *Heroes*, was the figure of a grieving Captain America looming above the smoking site of the World Trade Center.

Created as a symbol of freedom, American ideals, and hope on the verge of America's war against the Axis powers, Captain America is now comics' symbol of the struggle of free people against terrorism. One of Marvel's oldest heroes, the spirit of Captain America keeps him forever young.

AMAZING FANTASY
APPROVED BY THE COMICS CODE AUTHORITY
MC
12¢
15 AUG
INTRODUCING SPIDER MAN
THOUGH THE WORLD MAY MOCK PETER PARKER, THE TIMID TEEN AGER...
...IT WILL SOON MARVEL AT THE AWESOME MIGHT OF SPIDER-MAN!
ALSO IN THIS ISSUE:
AN IMPORTANT MESSAGE TO YOU, FROM THE EDITOR--ABOUT THE NEW AMAZING!

THE AMAZING SPIDER-MAN

HOW AN AWKWARD ORPHAN TEENAGER BECAME A POP ICON

When most people think of Super Heroes, they think of perfect individuals who lead perfect lives. They're handsomer than other people; they're more powerful than other people. Some of these heroes, like Batman, are fabulously wealthy. Others, like Superman, act shy, timid, and unlucky in love in their secret identities, but readers know that they're really completely the opposite. Moreover, these heroes inevitably triumph, and everybody in their fictional cities loves and admires them. This is what Super Heroes were like until the early 1960s.

Who back then would have dreamed that Superman and Batman would someday be rivaled in popularity by a skinny kid from New York City's outer boroughs who sewed his own costume together? Yes, he was stronger than ordinary people, but not as strong as many of his enemies, who often left him beaten and defeated. Not only could this kid not afford his own version of the Batmobile, he often had trouble making his rent. He didn't just pretend not to fit in with his social circle; this kid really was an outsider. His foster father and his first true love both died, and each time he was partly to blame. And no matter how hard he tried to help other people, they continued to distrust him.

This is Peter Parker, the "Amazing Spider-Man," the most unlikely of heroes who, nonetheless, has become not only Marvel Comics' flagship character, but the star of novels, videogames, television shows, and two blockbuster movies with still more to come.

Spider-Man debuted in 1962, less than a year after editor/writer Stan Lee and artist/co-plotter Jack Kirby had launched Marvel's revolution of Super Hero comics with *Fantastic Four* #1. Lee and Kirby had been working in comics since the "Golden Age" of the 1940s, when the first wave of Super Heroes was created. But following the post–World War II sales decline in Super Hero comics, virtually the entire genre had vanished by the early 1950s.

ALTHOUGH *AMAZING FANTASY* #15 WAS THE END OF ONE MARVEL SERIES, IT WAS ALSO THE BEGINNING FOR A BRAND NEW TYPE OF SUPER HERO.

RIGHT: *FANTASTIC FOUR* #1 MARKED A TURNING POINT FOR MARVEL AND FOR STAN LEE.

OPPOSITE: AS PART OF STAN LEE'S VISION FOR MORE REALISTIC CHARACTERS, THE FANTASTIC FOUR ARGUED WITH EACH OTHER JUST LIKE NORMAL PEOPLE.

In 1956, however, editor Julius Schwartz began revamping "Golden Age" Super Hero characters for a new generation of readers at Marvel's principal competitor, the company now known as DC Comics. Thus began the "Silver Age" of Super Hero comics. Schwartz's relaunches proved so successful that in 1961 Marvel publisher Martin Goodman directed Stan Lee to devise a new Super Hero team to compete with Schwartz's Justice League of America.

As Lee has frequently recounted, he had wearied of writing comic books, which were then considered solely a children's medium, and was on the verge of quitting. Entering middle age, Lee had long dreamed of writing more serious fiction. As Lee tells the story, his wife urged him to start writing the kinds of comics he would want to read himself.

This was an epiphany for Lee, and it was also a turning point in the history of American comics. Lee began asking himself what it would be like if Super Heroes existed in the real world. What would normal people do with superhuman powers? How would leading a career as a superpowered adventurer complicate a person's relationship with his friends, family, and colleagues? How would the world react to super-powerful individuals abruptly appearing in their midst?

These were some of the questions underlying Lee and Kirby's co-creation of the "Fantastic Four," the first modern Marvel Super Heroes, in 1961. The team members quarreled amongst themselves. The adult men, Reed Richards and Ben Grimm, were each attracted to their female colleague, Sue Storm. The fourth member, Johnny Storm, was a hotheaded, rebellious teen. As early as the second issue, the Fantastic Four were wrongly accused of crimes, and the fickle public turned against them. Surely most startling to readers was the transformation of Ben Grimm from a normal human being into the "Thing," a monster with superhuman strength. In the first *Fantastic Four* people were shocked and frightened when they saw him. Both angry and morose over his fate, the Thing felt alienated from the human race, even as he devoted his life to helping to protect them. Lee and Kirby had demonstrated that having superpowers could be a curse. They followed the Thing with an even more monstrous anti-hero, the "Incredible Hulk," in 1962.

Apart from these early Super Hero comics, Marvel circa 1962 was best known for its anthology titles, consisting of science fiction and supernatural tales often involving immense monsters of the sort young readers could see in low budget sci-fi movies of that time. Among these comics series was a title that began in 1961 as Amazing Adventures, which later changed its name to Amazing Adult Fantasy, featuring such monsters as "Tim Boo Ba."

After the title change, all of the stories were collaborations by Stan Lee with artist Steve Ditko, who also illustrated all the covers. But this comic book was unsuccessful, and issue #15 was scheduled to be its last.

Lee, in his creative prime and determined to experiment still further with reinventing the Super Hero concept, decided the lead feature for the final issue of Amazing Adult Fantasy would be the origin story of a new Super Hero, the Amazing Spider-Man.

Martin Goodman disliked the name, arguing that nobody liked spiders. Stan Lee had named this new character after the "Spider," a masked vigilante who in the 1930s had starred in a series of pulp novels much like those of his more celebrated contemporary, the "Shadow."

Originally Lee assigned his top artist, Jack Kirby, to draw Spider-Man, yet Lee was dissatisfied with the results. Kirby, co-creator of Captain America, is rightly renowned for drawing idealized, muscular, heroic figures, but in this case Lee wanted something different: not a powerful, mature adult, but a young, skinny

ABOVE: STEVE DITKO'S RENDERING OF SPIDER-MAN WAS THE PERFECT FIT FOR STAN LEE'S VISION OF A SKINNY, AWKWARD TEENAGER WITH SUPERPOWERS.

OPPOSITE: THE OPENING PAGE OF THE SPIDER-MAN ORIGIN STORY INTRODUCED READERS TO A VERY DIFFERENT TYPE OF SUPER HERO.

teenager with superpowers. In this and many other ways, Spider-Man would break the conventional mold of Super Heroes.

So Lee tapped Steve Ditko to draw the first Spider-Man story. Like Kirby, Ditko is a consummate master of comics storytelling who endowed action scenes with dynamic energy that made many competing comics of that time look dull by comparison. Yet Ditko did not draw idealized heroic figures; his leading men and women were not even conventionally handsome. Instead they looked ordinary, realistic, and believable, and that was the point Stan Lee wanted to make about Spider-Man and his supporting cast. Peter Parker, the boy who became Spider-Man, was an everyman who happened to acquire superpowers. Whereas Kirby could create a dazzling Manhattan cityscape, Ditko portrayed the more mundane New York in which Peter Parker lived: the middleclass home in Forest Hills, Queens, the local public high school, and the back alleys where Spider-Man contended with muggers and other lowlifes. Whereas Kirby could magnificently draw the Fantastic Four's exploits on other planets, Ditko was highly effective in depicting the shadowed New York underworld in which Spider-Man often found himself: it was at once pedestrian and sinister.

Moreover, whereas Kirby's heroes might soar through the air like the Mighty Thor, Ditko endowed Spider-Man with a quirkier way of moving: he scurried up walls like a real spider. In costume, Ditko's Spider-Man was both human and strangely bug-like. Perhaps this was appropriate for a story for Amazing Adult Fantasy, whose stock-in-trade—although plummeting—was aliens and monsters.

So the Amazing Spider-Man made his first appearance on the cover of the final issue of Amazing Adult Fantasy, which had changed its name yet again to Amazing Fantasy for issue #15, dated August 1962. Fittingly, the cover was a collaboration between the two most important artists of Marvel's Silver Age: Jack Kirby penciled it, and Steve Ditko inked it. The Spider-Man story was scripted by Lee and illustrated by Ditko, and it took up nearly half the book; the rest consisted not of Super Hero stories but of more typical Amazing Adult Fantasy tales such as "Man in the Mummy Case" and "There Are Martians Among Us."

The famous opening page of "Spider-Man" showed the bespectacled protagonist, Peter Parker, not front and center but standing in the background, his sadness palpable. In the foreground were the "cool kids" of Midtown High School: one was Flash Thompson, football player, big man on campus, and bully, and the other a blonde girl, whose name was revealed in future issues,

SPIDER-MAN!
LIKE COSTUMED HEROES? CONFIDENTIALLY, WE IN THE COMIC MAG BUSINESS REFER TO THEM AS "LONG UNDERWEAR CHARACTERS"! AND, AS YOU KNOW, THEY'RE A DIME A DOZEN! BUT, WE THINK YOU MAY FIND OUR SPIDERMAN JUST A BIT... DIFFERENT!
SAY, GANG, WE NEED ONE MORE GUY FOR THE DANCE! HOW ABOUT PETER PARKER OVER THERE?
ARE YOU KIDDIN'? THAT BOOKWORM WOULDN'T KNOW A CHA-CHA FROM A WALTZ!
PETER PARKER? HE'S MIDTOWN HIGH'S ONLY PROFESSIONAL WALLFLOWER!
Stan Lee & S. DITKO
1

was spoiled little rich girl Liz Allan. Flash, Liz, and their clique were entertaining themselves by mocking "bookworm" Peter Parker. They would not be caught dead associating with him.

Over the decades it has become fashionable, even among Spider-Man writers, to refer to the fifteen-year-old Peter Parker as a "nerd" or "geek"—words not commonly used then—as if they were taking Flash's side. Stan Lee, though, was considerably more sympathetic and respectful toward Peter. Lee and Ditko portrayed Flash and his friends as attractive, but also as shallow and cruel. In contrast, Peter was quietly admirable, a brilliant, dedicated student who was a good son to the elderly couple who raised him.

When Peter was a baby his parents died, and his father's brother, Uncle Ben, and his wife, Aunt May, brought him up as if he were their own son. (Years later Lee would reveal that Peter's parents were

BELOW: THE FAMOUS SPIDER BITE.

OPPOSITE: PETER PARKER'S NEW POWERS WERE CONFIRMED WHEN HE LEAPED OUT OF THE WAY OF A SPEEDING CAR.

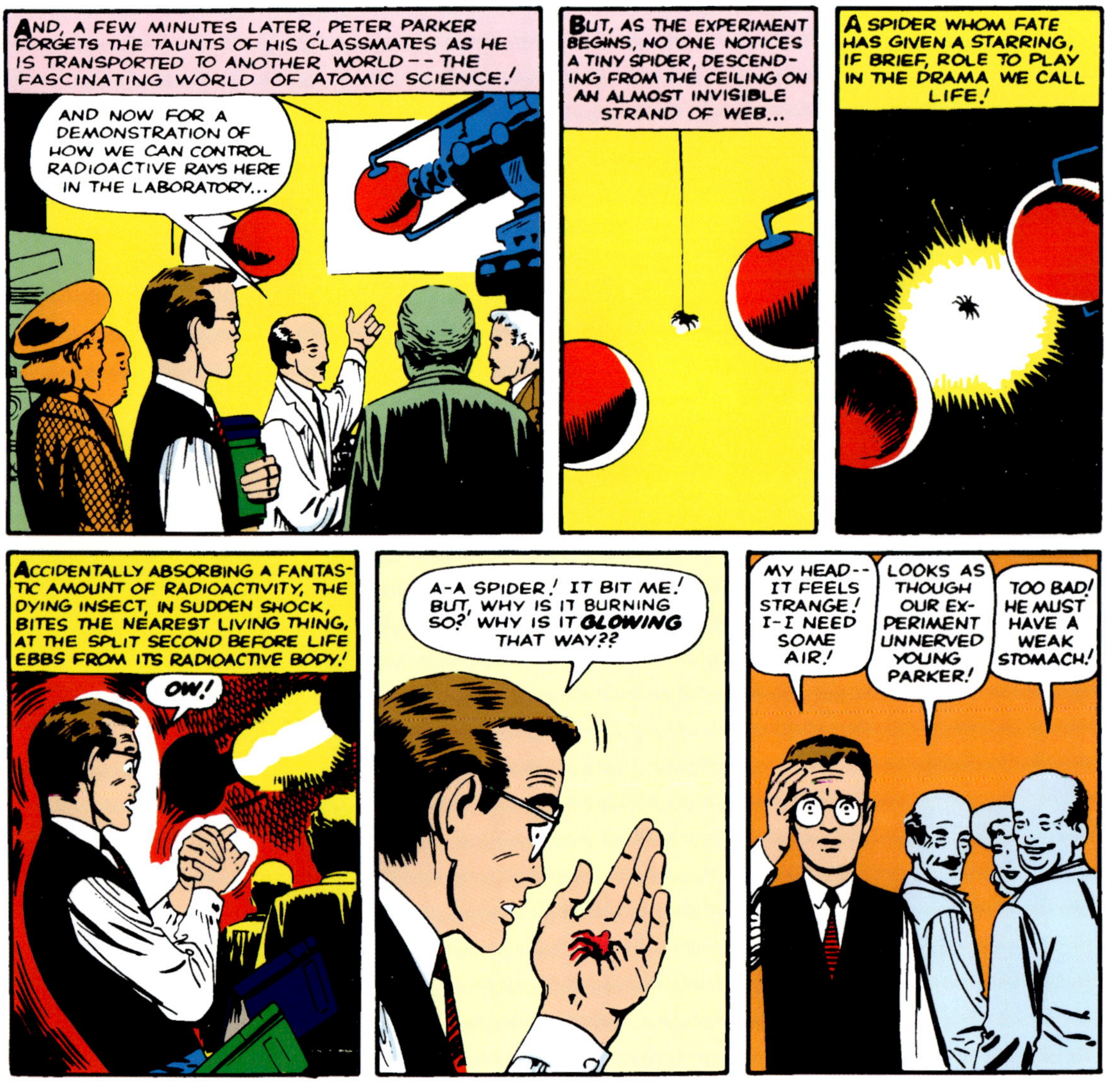

themselves heroes—intelligence operatives killed on a government mission.) Lee and Ditko especially idealized Uncle Ben, a wise, serene figure who taught Peter that "with great power must also come—great responsibility." People who quote this maxim often leave out the "must," but it is an essential word: to Ben, if one gained the power to accomplish great things, it was one's duty to take responsibility for helping other people.

One fateful day, Peter went on a school excursion to a local atomic physics laboratory. There a spider was exposed to atomic radiation. Fears of nuclear war were rampant in 1962. The Cold War would reach its apex with the Cuban Missile Crisis in October of that year, less than two months after the spider-bitten teen Super Hero made his debut. Science fiction of the period voiced people's fears that radiation could kill or horribly mutate its victims. But Stan Lee and his collaborators used it as a means of bestowing superpowers, as if it were a modern form of magic.

So it was that the irradiated spider bit the unsuspecting Peter Parker, who then killed it with a blow of his hand. Soon afterward Peter discovered that he had grown many times stronger, that he could leap great heights, and that he could even cling to walls with his hands and feet. He realized that somehow he had been transformed by the bite of the glowing spider.

In co-creating Spider-Man, Stan Lee was drawing on the idea that insects can lift objects that are many times their own weight. (Think of a jungle ant carrying a large leaf.) Peter Parker had gained the "proportional strength of a spider" and other arachnid abilities as well.

How did he cling to walls? Stan Lee never really explained it. Later, Mark Gruenwald, editor of *The Official Handbook of the Marvel Universe*, decided that Peter's body created an electrostatic effect that caused the molecules of his hands and feet to adhere to solid objects. (In the recent *Spider-Man* movies, tiny claws were shown to emerge from his hands, allowing him to cling to walls.)

Remarkably, Peter also discovered that he had developed a "sixth sense" that alerted him to danger by giving him a tingling sensation. Surely everyone has had the experience of being about to swat a fly or some other insect, when the bug quickly scurries out of the way. Presumably this is what inspired Stan Lee to give Peter his "spider-sense." In the comics this has traditionally been treated as a psychic ability. Peter's spider-sense alerts him if someone is coming up behind him to attack, but not if the unseen person approaching him

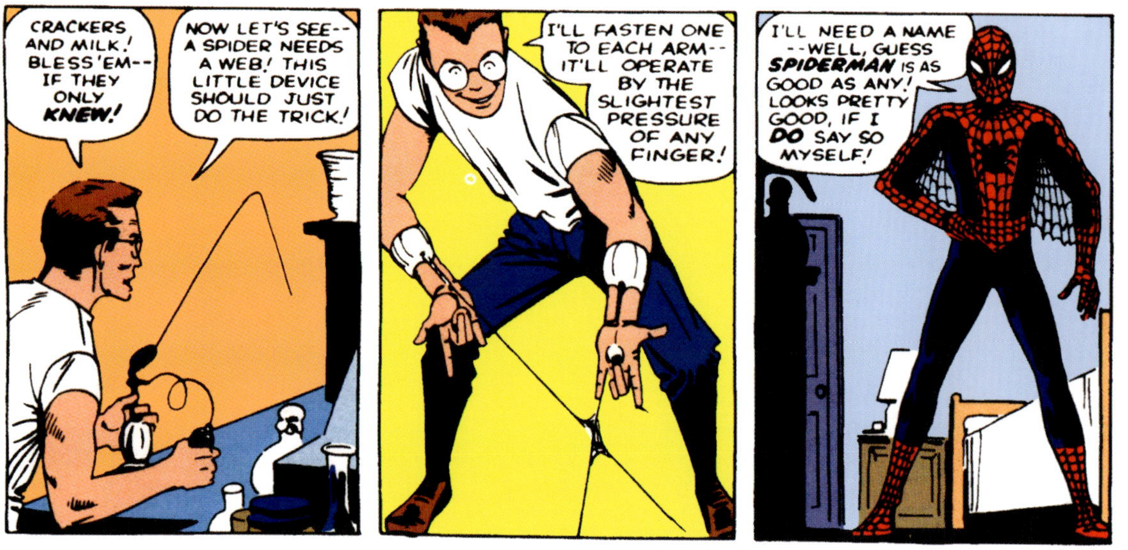

is a friend. In the movies, however, spider-sense seems to mean that Peter has superhumanly fast reactions: he can get out of the way of an adversary's fist the instant he glimpses it.

There was one ability Peter did not get from the spider's bite: the ability to create his own webbing. In a perhaps overly coincidental plot twist, Lee revealed that Peter was so brilliant at science that once he set his mind to the task he was able to concoct artificial "web fluid" virtually overnight. He devised apparatus that enabled him to shoot the fluid from his gloves; once the streams made contact with the air, they would solidify into "webbing" that was strong enough to bear his own weight. Hence, rather than flying through the air, Spider-Man swung from building to building on strands of webbing like an urban Tarzan. The webbing would dissolve within an hour. (In fact, this was why Peter didn't sell his formula and make a fortune: the webbing's impermanence made it impractical for any uses beyond superheroing.)

In traditional Super Hero stories, when a person gained superpowers he unselfishly decided to use them to fight crime and rescue people from danger. But Lee and Ditko were not doing a traditional Super Hero story. How would a real American teenager react to suddenly gaining super-powers? That's right: he would use them to get rich and famous.

Still shy enough to wear a makeshift mask to hide his identity, Peter tested his new powers by fighting "Crusher" Hogan, a wrestler who took on all comers. The disguised Peter easily bested his opponent, impressing an agent watching in the audience, who made Peter an offer.

Here is another convention of Super Hero comics that Stan Lee questioned: Why do Super Heroes wear those costumes, anyway? Lee came up with the answer: Peter created the Spider-Man persona as a publicity gimmick for his new show business career. Enabled by his superpowers to perform astounding athletic feats, Spider-Man became an immediate media sensation. He was the Super Hero as superstar.

His true identity hidden by his mask, the shy, introverted Peter Parker now felt free to indulge a side of his personality he had long kept buried. As Spider-Man he was brash and extroverted. He was also self-centered and egotistical. Following a television appearance, Spider-Man saw a guard pursuing a thief through a studio corridor. With his powers, Spider-Man could easily have stopped the thief, but he couldn't be bothered and let him escape.

Soon afterwards, Peter Parker returned home to learn of a tragedy that, even more than the spider's bite, irrevocably changed the course of his life. Police told Peter that a burglar had broken into his house and killed his Uncle Ben.

Nearly hysterical with rage, Peter changed into his Spider-Man costume and hunted down the fleeing murderer. Confronting him in a darkened warehouse, Spider-Man overcame the villain and finally got a

OPPOSITE: (TOP) CREATING WEB SHOOTERS WAS EASY FOR THE BRILLIANT PETER PARKER; (BOTTOM) PETER SELFISHLY LET A THIEF ESCAPE, AND HIS INACTION WOULD COME BACK TO HAUNT HIM.

BELOW: CRUSHER HOGAN WAS NO MATCH FOR PETER PARKER'S ARACHNID ABILITIES.

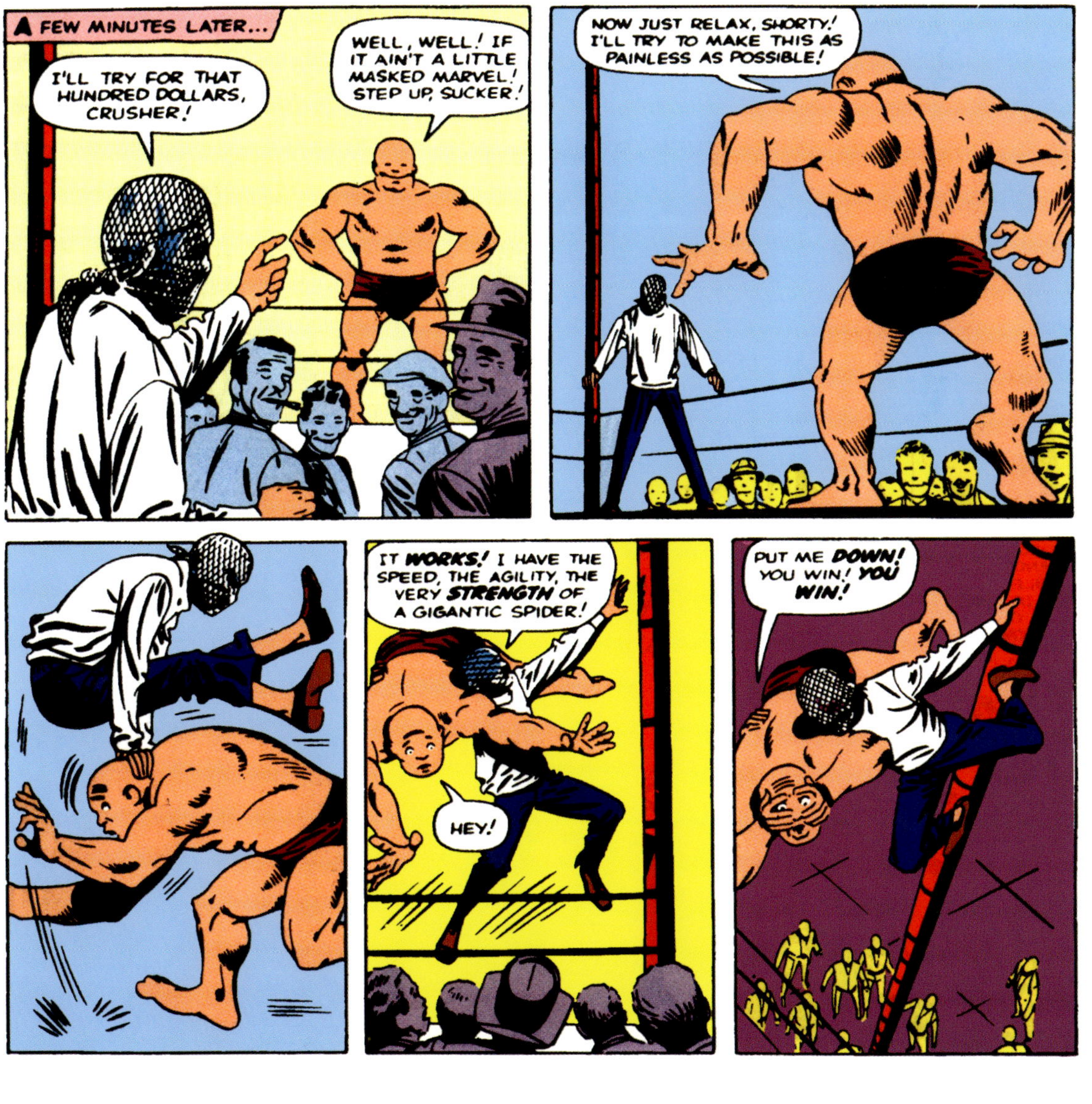

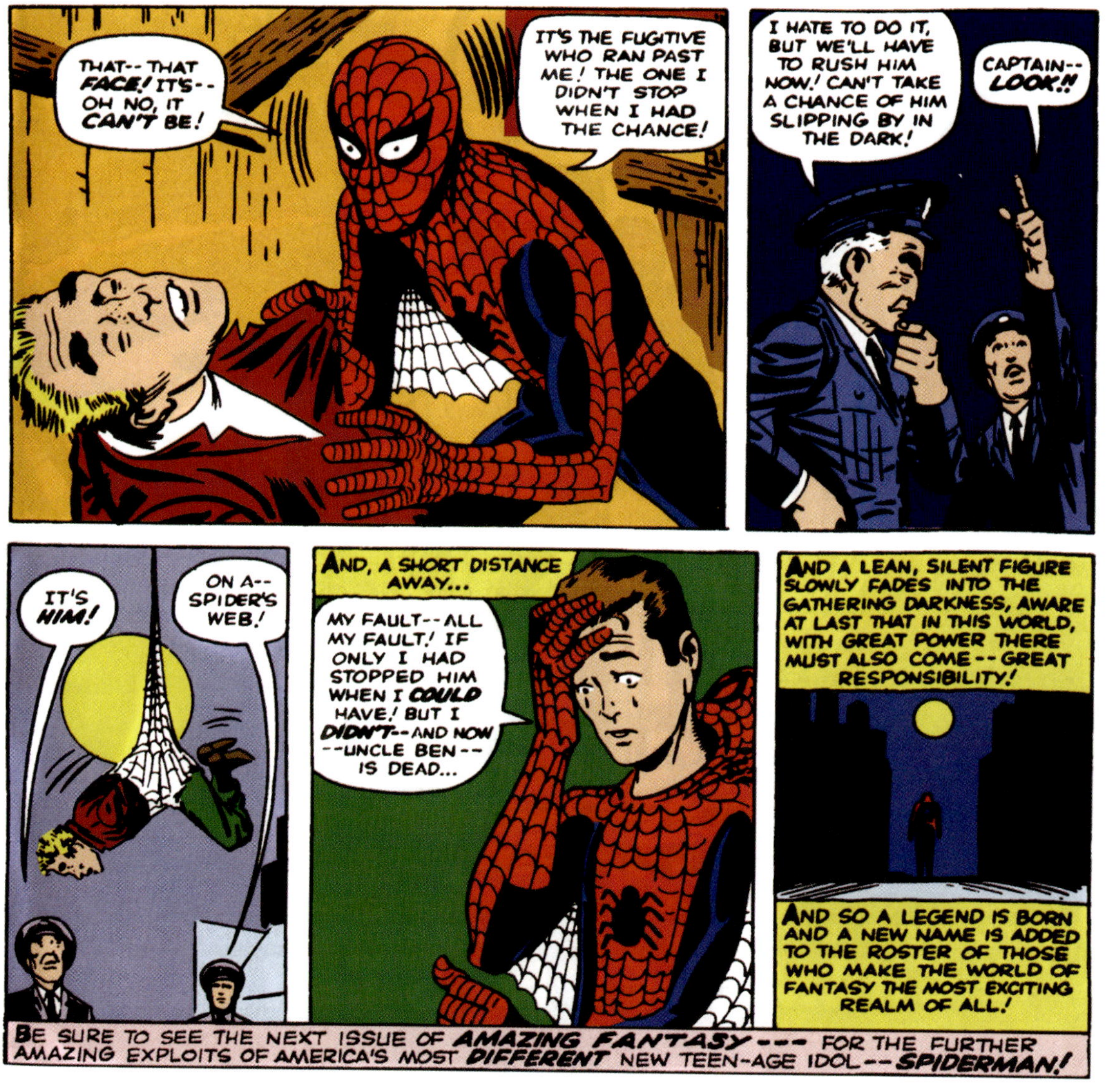

good look at him: it was the same thief whom he had allowed to escape at the television studio. Peter Parker was horrified: he was partly to blame for his beloved uncle's death.

This was an astonishing moment in the history of Super Hero comics. Spider-Man would not be motivated to become a costumed crime-fighter through sheer altruism, as Superman and Captain America were. Nor was he motivated by revenge, like Batman, whose parents were gunned down by a mugger. No, Spider-Man would become a Super Hero out of guilt. For the rest of his days, he would fight crime in order to expiate his own failure to prevent his uncle's murder. Spider-Man believed he could never again allow any innocent person to come to harm if he could prevent it.

This first Spider-Man story ended not in triumph, but with Ditko's haunting shot of Spider-Man trudging away, his shoulders slumped in depression. In his narration, Stan Lee wrote that Spider-Man recalled Uncle Ben's teaching: "With great power there must also come — great responsibility." That was the principle that would guide Spider-Man's life. It is also the most famous single line that Stan Lee has ever written and the key to understanding the underlying philosophy of the stories he wrote for Marvel in the 1960s.

Previously in comics, teenage Super Heroes were usually kid sidekicks, like Batman's "Robin the Boy Wonder," working with an older mentor. Stan Lee disliked the kid sidekick concept. When he co-created teen Super Heroes such as the original X-Men, they went into combat on their own, shouldering adult responsibilities. Peter Parker was Spider-Man, not Spider-Boy, and his saga would be that of a youth grappling with adult responsibilities and striving toward maturity.

Lee and Ditko's experiment proved successful, and though Amazing Fantasy was no more, the Amazing Spider-Man was awarded his own comic book; the first issue was dated March 1963.

In this issue's lead story, Spider-Man risked his life to save astronaut Colonel John Jameson from his plummeting spacecraft. Though Spider-Man proved successful, the Colonel's father was incensed. One of the series' most prominent characters, J. Jonah Jameson, the irascible publisher of the *Daily Bugle*, a fictional tabloid newspaper, thundered that Spider-Man, heretofore known as a showbiz celebrity, was merely a publicity hound, trying to steal attention away from true heroes like his astronaut son.

J. Jonah Jameson may not be a super-powered criminal, but he has justly been called Spider-Man's most implacable foe. Ever since issue #1, Jameson has kept up his barrage of assaults on Spider-Man's character, accusing him of being just as much of a criminal as the villains he fights.

As a result of Jameson's continual slanders, Spider-Man's show business career collapsed. With Uncle Ben dead, young Peter had to struggle to support himself and his frail, sickly Aunt May.

OPPOSITE: WHEN PETER DISCOVERED THAT HE COULD HAVE PREVENTED UNCLE BEN'S DEATH, HIS UNCLE'S NOW-FAMOUS AXIOM FINALLY BECAME CLEAR TO HIM.

ABOVE: THE *AMAZING SPIDER-MAN* #1.

BELOW: SPIDER-MAN SAVED COLONEL JOHN JAMESON'S SPACECRAFT, BUT MADE AN ENEMY IN THE COLONEL'S FATHER, J. JONAH JAMESON.

Even worse, the general public turned against Spider-Man, whom they had acclaimed only days before. By this story's close, Peter Parker felt himself just as alienated from society as those monsters, the Thing and the Hulk.

Yet the resourceful Peter found a way to turn Jameson's Spider-Man smear campaign to his own benefit. Jameson had mixed motives for his one-man media war. In one early issue, Jameson even realized that he was enviously seeking to tear down Spider-Man for being the hero he could never be himself. Jameson also realized that putting Spider-Man on the front page sold newspapers. So Peter Parker came up with the idea of using an automatic camera to take pictures of himself in action as Spider-Man and then sell them to Jameson. Thus this high school student ended up becoming one of the *Bugle*'s leading freelance photographers.

The scenes with Parker at the *Bugle* showed another side to Jameson's personality: he was perhaps Stan Lee's finest comedy character, an absurdly cheap, egotistical blowhard. Despite Jameson's volcanic temper, he became something of a father figure for Peter, and over time both Peter and the readers have grown fond of Jonah despite himself.

It was at the *Bugle* that Peter Parker met Jameson's young secretary, Betty Brant, who debuted in issue #4 (September 1963). She would be the series' leading lady during Steve Ditko's stint on the book, although the relationship between Peter and Betty never evolved beyond an endearing mutual crush.

Issue #1 featured the first of Lee and Ditko's long line of classic Spider-Man villains, one of the finest and most memorable rogues' galleries in comics. Again, Ditko's talents were the key. Whereas Jack Kirby would draw such imposing figures as Doctor Doom and Galactus for Fantastic Four, Ditko drew a gang of grotesques.

First came the Chameleon, an enemy spy who wore an eerie blank mask, concealing his head as if he were faceless. Appearing in issue #1 (April 1963), this master of disguise impersonated Spider-Man to commit his crimes, thereby turning the police against the young hero. Now Spider-Man truly was an outcast from society.

In issue #2 (May 1963), Lee and Ditko introduced the first great Spider-Man villain, the "Vulture": an elderly man with a bald, wizened head, who wore a winged costume that enabled him to fly. Spider-Man's battles with the Vulture became archetypal conflicts between youth and age.

Only one issue later (July 1963) came an even greater creation, "Doctor Octopus," yet another example of 1960s preoccupations with the dangers of atomic radiation. Dr. Otto Octavius was a squat, ugly man with thick glasses and a Moe Howard haircut, but he was also a genius in nuclear physics. Octavius had invented a harness, which he wore around his waist, that had four robotic arms he utilized for handling dangerous radioactive materials. Since the metal arms resembled an Octopus's tentacles, he was nicknamed Doctor Octopus. Some of the

OPPOSITE: (TOP) PETER WAS SMART ENOUGH TO REALIZE THAT J. JONAH JAMESON WOULD PAY TOP DOLLAR FOR PHOTOS OF SPIDER-MAN; (BOTTOM) THE VULTURE FIRST APPEARED IN ISSUE #2.

BELOW: IN ISSUE #3 A RADIOACTIVE EXPLOSION FUSED DOCTOR OCTAVIOUS'S MECHANICAL ARMS TO HIS BODY.

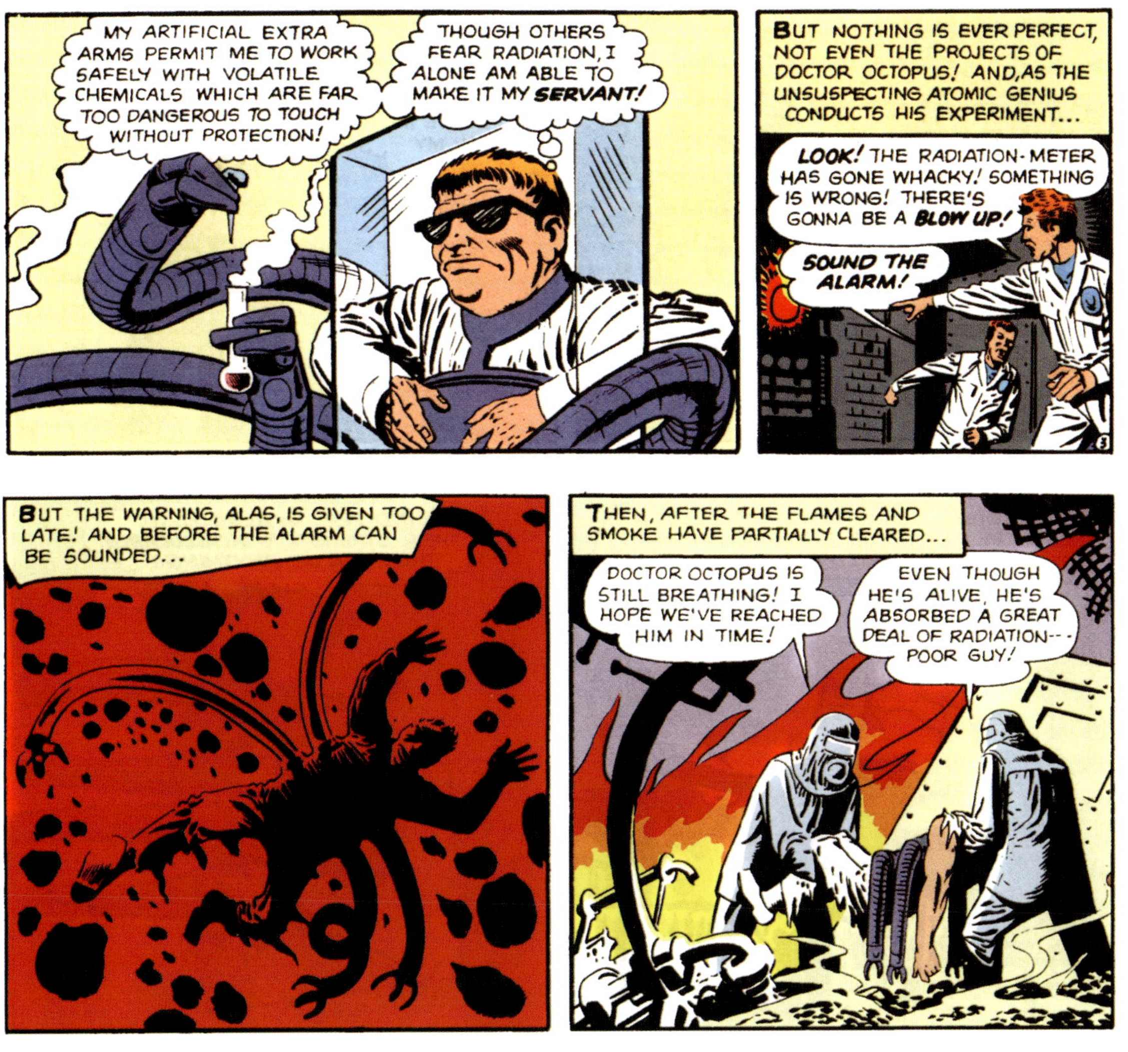

RIGHT: DOCTOR OCTUPUS'S NEWFOUND ABILITIES REVEALED THE DARK SIDE OF HIS PERSONALITY.

OPPOSITE: ISSUE #14, THE DEBUT OF THE GREEN GOBLIN.

radioactive material exploded and the results were incredible: The harness was fused to Octavius's body, and he discovered that he could now control the metal arms mentally. Furthermore, the explosion distorted Octavius's psyche, releasing an alternate evil personality. To this day the villainous Doctor Octopus remains one of Spider-Man's two leading archenemies.

But Lee and Ditko were far from through creating conflict. Next came the "Sandman," a common thug who was given the ability to turn his body to sand or to rock-hard granite through his exposure to atomic radiation (*Amazing Spider-Man* #4, September 1963). Dr. Curt Connors studied how certain reptiles could regenerate parts of their bodies in order to find a means of regrowing his missing arm; instead, he turned himself into the "Lizard," a marauding reptile with a sinister human intellect (issue #6, November 1963). An electric company employee working on a power line suffered an accident that turned him into "Electro," a criminal who generated electricity from his own body (issue #9, February 1964). The enigmatic "Mysterio" was a movie special effects designer who used technology to feign having supernatural powers (issue #12, June 1964).

In issue #14 the only rival to Doctor Octopus for the title of Spider-Man's foremost enemy made his debut. This was the "Green Goblin," a criminal mastermind whom Ditko designed as if he were a demon from a medieval woodcut. Instead of a witch's broomstick, the Goblin flew through the air on a one-man jet engine and fired sparkling bolts of energy from his gloves, as if casting spells. From the very first, the Green Goblin regarded Spider-Man as the principal obstacle to his goal of taking control of the New York criminal underworld. But who was the Goblin? Lee and Ditko made it clear that the Goblin was a human being in a grotesque costume, but shielded his true face from readers for two years.

The Goblin was followed by "Kraven the Hunter" (issue #15, August 1964), who prided himself on using his superhuman strength and hunter's wiles to capture the beasts of the jungle, and regarded Spider-Man as his ultimate target.

the AMAZING SPIDER-MAN
IND.
APPROVED BY THE COMICS CODE AUTHORITY
MARVEL COMICS GROUP 12¢
14 JULY
WOW!! JUST WAIT TILL YOU SEE "The GREEN GOBLIN!"
DOES THE GREEN GOBLIN LOOK CUTE TO YOU? DOES HE MAKE YOU WANT TO SMILE? WELL, FORGET IT! HE'S THE MOST SINISTER, MOST DANGEROUS FOE SPIDEY'S EVER FOUGHT!
GUEST-STARRING NONE OTHER THAN THAT RAMPAGING POWERHOUSE, THE INCREDIBLE HULK!
NO! YOU'RE NOT SEEING THINGS! THESE REALLY ARE THE EVIL ENFORCERS, BACK AGAIN TO GANG UP ON OUR OL' WEB-SPINNER!

BELOW: COMMISSIONING THE CREATION OF THE SCORPION WAS ONLY THE FIRST OF J. JONAH JAMESON'S MANY ATTEMPTS TO GET RID OF SPIDER-MAN.

OPPOSITE: (TOP) PETER'S OBLIVIOUSNESS INTRIGUED CLASSMATE GWEN STACY AND SHE EVENTUALLY BECAME HIS FIRST LOVE INTEREST; (BOTTOM) ISSUE #33, THE FINEST OF THE STAN LEE AND STEVE DITKO COLLABORATIONS.

Even J. Jonah Jameson tried his hand at capturing Spider-Man, first by commissioning the transformation of a private eye he had hired into the superhumanly strong "Scorpion" (issue #20, January 1965), and then through Professor Spencer Smythe's "Spider-Slayer" robot (issue #25, June 1965), the first of many mechanized enemies to come.

The life of Peter Parker was beset by troubles, but he found an emotional release as Spider-Man. Perhaps Peter could not overcome his everyday problems, but Spider-Man usually triumphed over his nemeses. Not only did Spider-Man physically overcome his opponents, but while they blustered threats, he verbally cut them down to size with his jokes. Spider-Man proved to be the perfect vehicle for Stan Lee's sharp, witty dialogue.

In most comic books and strips the characters never age; Charlie Brown and Little Orphan Annie will remain children forever. But again

Stan Lee overturned convention when Peter Parker graduated from high school and started college studies at Empire State University, obviously based on Manhattan's New York University. Some comics professionals now regard this development as a mistake. But in the mid-1960s, after the ups and downs of the comics industry in the past, Stan Lee had no reason to believe that Spider-Man would still be published four decades later. Later Marvel writers greatly slowed down Peter Parker's aging process, but by now he seems to be at least in his mid-twenties.

Flash Thompson, who ironically turned out to be Spider-Man's most loyal fan, also went to E.S.U., where he and "puny Parker" finally became friends. The change of venue allowed Lee and Ditko to give Peter some new classmates: Harry Osborn, son of wealthy industrialist Norman Osborn, and Gwen Stacy, daughter of a police captain (issue #31, December 1965). Initially Harry and Gwen regarded Peter with disdain, but Harry would become Peter's best friend, and Gwen would prove to be his first true love. Meanwhile, Aunt May kept trying to introduce Peter to a girl named Mary Jane, whom readers never saw but whom Peter was certain would be plain and boring.

Like Jack Kirby, Steve Ditko increasingly took over the plotting of the stories, which Stan Lee, busy editing the entire Marvel line, continued to script. The peak of the Lee-Ditko collaboration was "The Final Chapter" (issue #33, February 1966). Following a battle with Doctor Octopus, Spider-Man was pinned beneath tons of fallen machinery as Doc Ock's hideout began to flood with water. Ditko's mastery of depicting body language combined perfectly with Lee's ability to evoke personality and

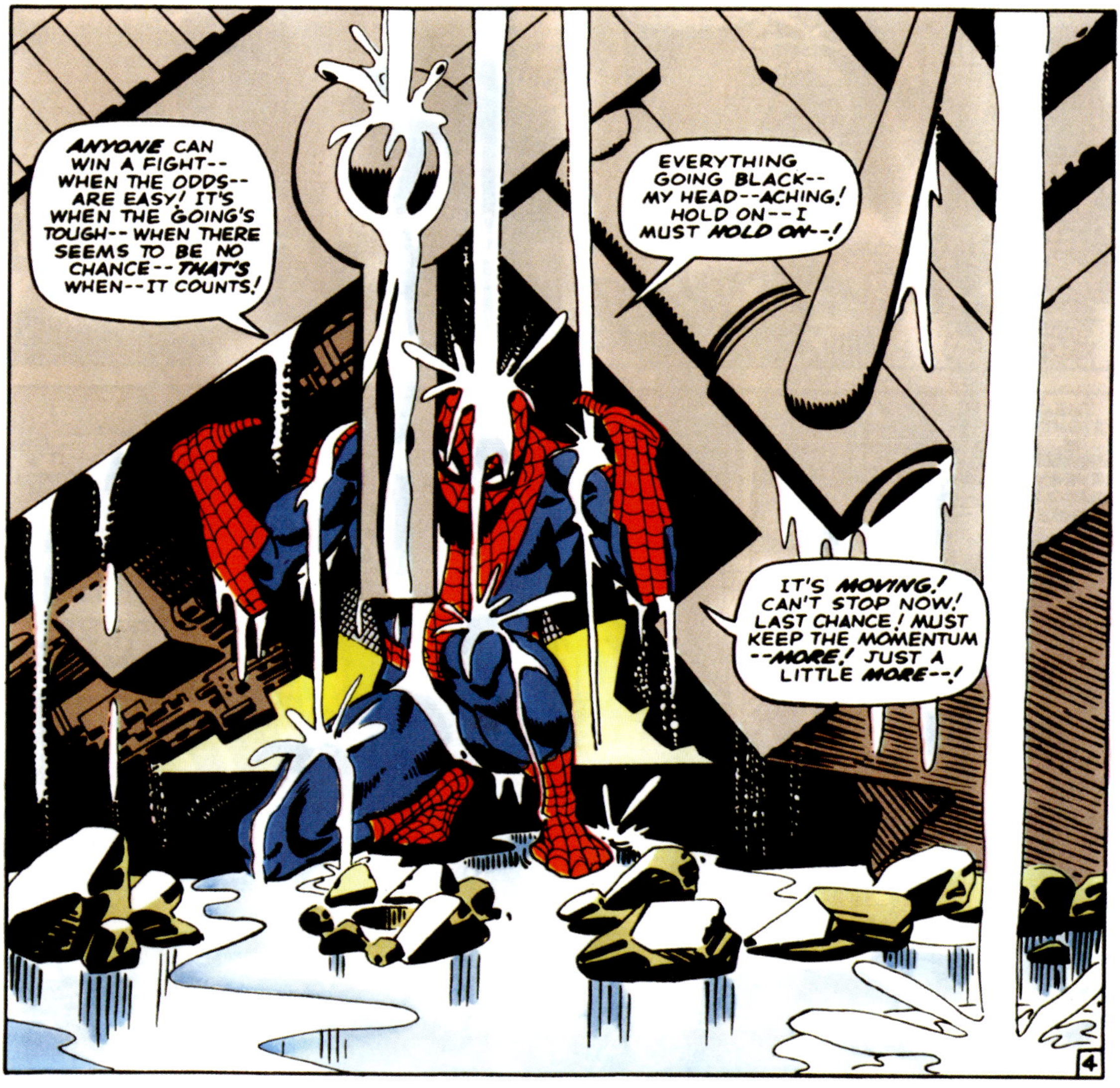

drama through dialogue as Spider-Man struggled against the overwhelming weight, inspired by his duty to save Aunt May, who lay on the brink of death in a hospital. Finally, Spider-Man threw off the weight in a powerful full-page panel—a triumphant example of comics storytelling at its greatest.

Yet Steve Ditko wearied of his collaboration with Stan Lee, preferring to work on his own, and quit both Spider-Man and Marvel with issue #38 (July 1966). The classic Lee-Ditko run on Spider-Man, the foundation of the series, lasted a mere four years.

Ditko's unique artistic style was irreplaceable, so Stan Lee turned to a very different artist to succeed him: John Romita Sr., who took over the series with issue #39 (August 1966). Romita had considerable experience in romance comics, and so, inevitably, his Peter Parker was much handsomer than Ditko's thin, plain version. Lee initially resisted this new look but soon accepted it, and it has been argued that it fit Peter's increasing maturity in his college years.

Lee and Romita's Spider-Man collaboration began with a bang—a two-part story revealing that the Green Goblin was Harry's father, the forbiddingly stern business mogul Norman Osborn (issues #39–40, August to September 1966).

Romita's background in romance comics meant that he was far more skilled than Ditko at drawing beautiful women. Lee and Romita focused increasingly on the building romance between Peter and the now-gorgeous Gwen Stacy. Moreover, Lee seized the opportunity to have Romita reveal the face of the mysterious Mary Jane Watson, who proved to be a dazzling redhead (issue #42, November 1966). Whereas Lee and Romita put Gwen on the proverbial pedestal as an idealized ingénue, they presented Mary Jane as a saucy, witty, fun-loving extrovert. "Face it, tiger," she famously told Peter when they first met, "you just hit the jackpot." Lee and Romita regarded Gwen as the perfect woman for Peter, but Mary Jane was a far more vivid personality.

Lee and Romita's peak as a team came with a landmark story in issue #50, "Spider-Man No More." The burden of all his sufferings

OPPOSITE: IN A QUINT-ESSENTIAL MARVEL MOMENT, SPIDER-MAN CONJURED MORE POWER THAN READERS THOUGHT HE WAS CAPABLE OF AND ESCAPED FROM BEING PINNED UNDERNEATH TONS OF MACHINERY.

BELOW: PETER WAS SHOCKED TO LEARN THAT HIS BEST FRIEND'S FATHER WAS THE GREEN GOBLIN.

FALSE FATHERS

Since the Spider-Man series is about a young man grappling with the responsibilities of adulthood, it is no surprise that Peter Parker has dealt with a gallery of symbolic father figures. Some are benevolent: Uncle Ben, Captain Stacy, and Daily Bugle editor Joe "Robbie" Robertson (one of the first important African-American supporting characters in comics). Another is oppressive: J. Jonah Jameson. And two are downright evil: Doctor Octopus and Norman Osborn, the original Green Goblin.

In an example of Stan Lee and Steve Ditko's sense of irony, Peter's frail, elderly Aunt May long considered Spider-Man to be the menace that Jameson claimed he was. But she liked Doctor Octopus, whom she met in *Amazing Spider-Man Annual* #1 (1964), believing his tentacles to be newfangled sorts of prosthetic arms. She even took him in as a boarder after Peter moved out (*Amazing Spider-Man* #54, November 1967).

Lee's successor as Spider-Man writer, Gerry Conway, took the situation even further. Learning that May was the heir to a nuclear power plant, Doctor Octopus courted her and proposed marriage. Since Aunt May was effectively Peter's foster mother, Doc Ock would have become his foster father! Luckily, Spider-Man interrupted the wedding ceremony before they could be legally married in a story aptly titled "My Uncle—My Enemy?" (*Amazing Spider-Man* #134, April 1974).

In his second Spider-Man movie, Sam Raimi extended the theme by introducing Otto Octavius as a kindly mentor to Peter before he suffered the accident that distorted his mind, turning him into a father figure out to kill his son, Spider-Man.

Norman Osborn's stern, insensitive treatment of his son Harry was a sharp contrast to Ben Parker's paternal love for Peter. Just as Spider-Man lives by Uncle Ben's famous maxim about power and responsibility, so too Harry carried on in his sinister father's tradition. After the original Green Goblin (seemingly) died in combat, Harry, slipping into insanity, became the new Green Goblin, out for revenge against his father's supposed killer, Spider-Man.

It was as if the Green Goblin could not die, even if the individuals wearing his mask could. Over the years several others would assume the guise of the Goblin, even Harry's psychiatrist! Another criminal mastermind who found a cache of Norman Osborn's weaponry altered the original Goblin's costume to become a new villain, the "Hobgoblin."

Eventually Norman Osborn turned up alive, having lain low in Europe for years. It was explained that the serum that granted him superhuman strength had also enabled him to recover from the seemingly fatal wound he had received. By now Harry was dead, but Norman considered him an unworthy weakling. Instead, the original Green Goblin now intended either to make Spider-Man his heir or to destroy him.

In the first Spider-Man movie Sam Raimi pursued the same angle. His version of Norman Osborn clearly preferred the brilliant Peter Parker to his own underachieving son; as the Green Goblin he sought to persuade Spider-Man to join forces with him. In the end, the movie Goblin died the same way that the comics' version once "perished." But in the second movie Norman Osborn's ghost—real or only imagined?—haunts Harry, who seems likely to follow his own comics counterpart's path to becoming "Green Goblin II."

AUNT MAY'S AFFECTION FOR DOC OCK'S ODD ARMS TURNED HIM INTO A TWISTED SORT OF PATERNAL FIGURE, A NUANCE THAT WOULD ALSO CHARACTERIZE PETER PARKER'S RELATIONSHIP WITH HIS OTHER ARCHENEMY, THE GREEN GOBLIN.

over the previous forty-nine issues finally proved too much for Peter Parker, who decided that his Spider-Man career had wrecked his life. So he threw his costume in a trashcan and abandoned his Super Hero identity. In a pattern that would be repeated time and again over the years, Peter eventually realized yet again that "with great power must come great responsibility" and resumed his role as Spider-Man. This is the archetypal Spider-Man story, so it is no wonder that director Sam Raimi used it as the basis of the second Spider-Man movie, going so far as to recreate Romita's iconic image of Peter walking away from the costume in the trash can.

Issue #50 also introduced the latest of Spider-Man's classic nemeses, the "Kingpin of Crime," a criminal overlord who subsequently became the leading villain in writer/artist Frank Miller's run on Daredevil and in the recent *Daredevil* movie.

By now the Amazing Spider-Man was the top-selling comic in Marvel's increasingly successful line. But despite the book's commercial success, Lee never forgot the tragic aspects of the Spider-Man series. In issue #90 (November 1970), Gwen's father, Captain Stacy, who had become a paternal figure for Peter as well, died heroically saving a child from falling debris during a battle between Spider-Man and Doctor Octopus; as usual, the public, Jameson, and even Gwen wrongly blamed Spider-Man for Captain Stacy's death.

At that time the comic book business operated under a self-imposed "Comics Code," which, among other things, forbade any mention of drugs. Persuaded that he could use comics to help fight drug addiction, Lee and Marvel defied the code by publishing a three-part Spider-Man story (issues #96–98, May to July 1971), in which Harry Osborn fell seriously ill as the result of taking unidentified pills provided

BELOW: THE FAMOUS MEETING OF PETER PARKER AND MARY JANE WATSON.

OPPOSITE: THE FINAL PAGE OF "SPIDER-MAN NO MORE."

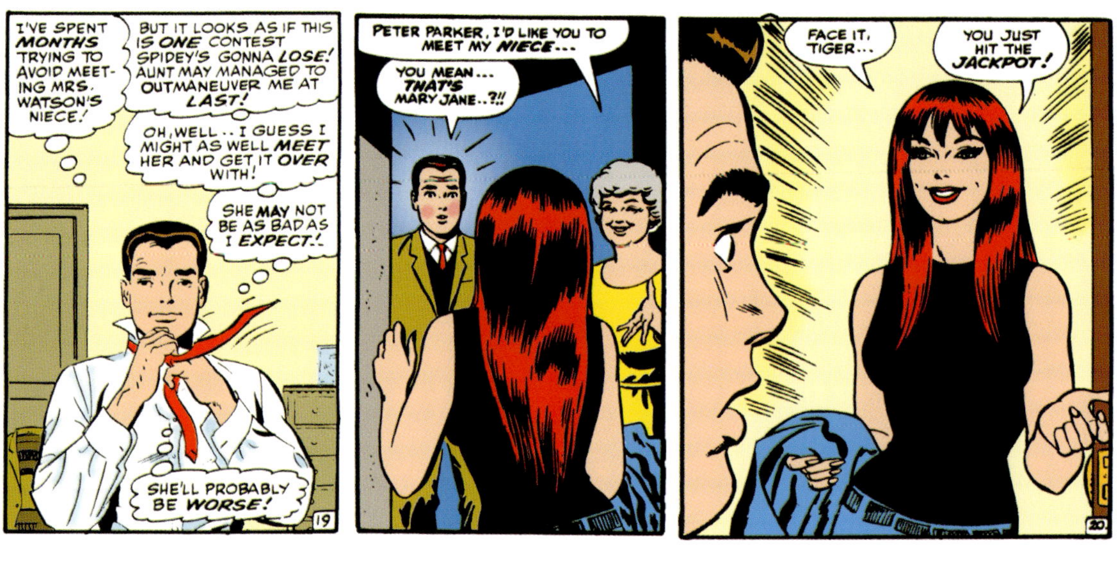

I WAS JUST A YOUNG, UNTHINKING TEENAGER... WHEN I FIRST BECAME... SPIDER-MAN...
BUT, THE YEARS HAVE A WAY OF SLIPPING BY..OF CHANGING THE WORLD ABOUT US...
AND, EVERY BOY... SOONER OR LATER... MUST PUT AWAY HIS TOYS.. AND BECOME.. A MAN!
8

GWEN!
NO!
I'VE GOT TO CATCH HER--
FFFFTT
--STOP HER FALL BEFORE SHE HITS THE WATER!
I'VE GOT TO!
I'VE GOT TO!
DID IT!
SWIK!
SNAP!
SPIDER-POWERS, I LOVE YOU!
NOT ONLY AM I THE MOST DASHING HERO ON TWO LEGS--

LEFT: HARRY OSBORN'S STRUGGLE WITH DRUG ADDICTION CHANGED THE "COMICS CODE."

OPPOSITE: THE DEATH OF GWEN STACY.

by a pusher. The code changed as a result, paving the way for greater freedom of expression in mainstream comic books over the following decades.

Stan Lee continued to write the Amazing Spider-Man longer than any other series at Marvel. But as Marvel grew more successful, Lee increasingly devoted attention to his executive responsibilities, finally becoming publisher in 1972. *Amazing Spider-Man* #110 (July 1972) marked the end of Lee's remarkable run as the series' scripter; he was succeeded by new Marvel recruit Gerry Conway, who was then not much older than Peter Parker himself.

But Lee was hardly through with his most famous co-creation. Later in the 1970s Lee and Romita started a daily Spider-Man newspaper strip, one of the few successful adventure strips launched since 1970. Though Romita soon left the project, Stan Lee continues to script the strip today, which is now drawn by his brother, Larry Lieber.

Gerry Conway's run on Spider-Man will long be remembered for two landmark events. One was the introduction of a costumed vigilante called the "Punisher" (issue #129, February 1974), who would go on to his own comics series and two feature films. The other was the death of Gwen Stacy (issue #121, June 1973).

Originally John Romita's idea for shaking up the series' status quo, another Silver Age great, Gil Kane, drew the story. Knowing that Peter Parker was Spider-Man, the Green Goblin took his vengeance by throwing Gwen from the top of the Brooklyn Bridge. Spider-Man succeeded in catching her mid-fall, but the rescue was punctuated by the disturbing sound of her neck snapping. Was it the shock of the plunge that killed Gwen, or the sudden impact of being caught by her well-meaning rescuer?

In the ensuing battle between the vengeful Spider-Man and the Goblin in the following issue, the Goblin was impaled on the point of his own one-man flyer. The original Green Goblin was dead—or so it seemed for decades—and his son Harry, his mind warped by drugs, took his father's costume and subsequently sought vengeance on Spider-Man as the new Green Goblin. (Sam Raimi used elements of this story line in the Spider-Man movies, using Mary Jane as the Goblin's victim and opting for a happier ending.)

Even Stan Lee was upset by the death of Gwen, but Conway and Romita were continuing the theme that Lee had inaugurated with the death of Uncle Ben: Spider-Man's life was inseparable from tragedy. The death of the leading lady in a Super Hero series was unexpected and virtually unprecedented. Gwen's death was an unmistakable sign that the "Silver Age" of comics had ended. Retelling the story of Gwen's demise in their acclaimed series Marvels, writer Kurt Busiek and artist Alex Ross made clear that this is where the "darkening" of contemporary Super Hero comics began. Indeed, comics were no longer for little kids anymore.

Conway later tantalized readers with the possibility that Gwen was still alive. But this Gwen was only a clone, created by a costumed genetic engineer called the "Jackal," who grew a Spider-Man clone as well (issue #149, October 1975). The Spider-Clone was seemingly destroyed in that issue, but his creation would have unexpected repercussions more than fifteen years later.

Inevitably, as Spider-Man's popularity continued to rise, Marvel began creating new companion series for the Amazing Spider-Man. There was Marvel Team-Up (whose first issue was dated March 1972), which paired the web-slinger with other Marvel heroes, followed by Peter Parker, the Spectacular Spider-Man (December 1976), and many others, both mini-series and long-running monthlies.

Spider-Man first appeared on television as early as 1967 in an animated series produced by the legendary animation director Ralph Bakshi. There would be several other animated Spider-Man series over the decades, including, most recently, a computer-animated version produced for MTV. There was even a short-lived and disappointing live-action *Amazing Spider-Man* TV series in 1978 on CBS. A live-action Spider-Man also helped teach kids to read on the Children's Television Workshop's *The Electric Company* on PBS in the 1970s.

Among the many leading comics professionals who worked on Marvel's various Spider-Man comics in the 1970s and 1980s were writers Len Wein, Marv Wolfman, Archie Goodwin, Denny O'Neil, Roger Stern, Chris Claremont, J. M. DeMatteis, Louise Simonson, Tom DeFalco, Peter David, and David Michelinie. Major Spider-Man artists included John Romita's son, John Romita Jr., as well as Ross Andru, John Byrne, Frank Miller, Ron Frenz, Mike Zeck, and Mark Bagley.

In the course of Marvel's first major crossover series, Marvel Super Heroes Secret Wars (1984 to 1985), Spider-Man adopted a new black costume he found on an alien planet. Inevitably, Spider-Man returned to his familiar red and blue outfit. But the alien costume proved to be a living, intelligent creature, which bonded with a malcontent reporter, Eddie Brock, to become the menace called "Venom" (debuting in *Amazing Spider-Man* #99, April 1988), an evil foil to Spider-Man. Venom was co-created by writer David Michelinie and artist Todd McFarlane; the latter's style, combining dramatic power with a quirky cartoonish look, was like a contemporary analogue to Steve Ditko's. McFarlane became a comics superstar, and the first issue of a new Spider-Man series (August 1990) that he both wrote and drew became one of the best selling comic books of all time.

Mary Jane Watson disappeared from the Spider-Man books for a long time, but she eventually returned, and in 1984 writer Tom DeFalco gave the character a new twist: he revealed that she had discovered that Peter Parker was Spider-Man. DeFalco also gave her a back story, revealing that her "party girl" persona was her means of coping with the sadness of her childhood in a dysfunctional family. As a result, Mary Jane became Peter's trusted confidant. Gerry Conway later built on DeFalco's revelations in a graphic novel, *Spider-Man: Parallel Lives* (1989), in which he showed that Mary Jane, whose aunt lived next door to Peter's, had discovered he was Spider-Man on the night of Uncle Ben's death.

Mary Jane, it seemed, was Peter Parker's female counterpart: each hid their inner misery behind a wisecracking public persona. In other words, they were made for each other. Since Gwen's demise, Stan Lee had used Mary Jane as

OPPOSITE: FOR A SHORT TIME PETER PARKER DONNED A BLACK SPIDER-MAN COSTUME.

LEFT AND ABOVE: THE MARRIAGE OF PETER AND MARY JANE.

the female lead of the Spider-Man comic strip, and he eventually proposed that Peter and Mary Jane get married. So they did, simultaneously in both the comic strip and the comic book (*Amazing Spider-Man Annual* #21, 1987).

It seemed to be a good idea at the time, but years later editors and writers at Marvel believed that it had been a mistake. Spider-Man, in his own words, was "the hard-luck Harry" of the Super Hero world. Why, then, should he be married to a beautiful woman who had become a successful supermodel? Moreover, as often happens with long-running series, it was felt that the weight of decades of continuity had become too complicated and burdensome.

The solution they concocted in the 1990s was the controversial "Clone Saga." The idea was that the Spider-Man whose adventures readers had been following since 1975 was really the clone that the Jackal had created; the original Spider-Man, Peter Parker, had been living under the name "Ben Reilly." The Spider-Man writers dispatched the clone and his wife Mary Jane to Oregon to live happily ever after, and had "Ben" take over as Spider-Man.

The readers rebelled at being told that the last decade and a half of Spider-Man stories effectively did not count, and Marvel quickly reversed course. It was revealed that the married Peter Parker was indeed the original Spider-Man, and it was Ben who was the clone. The whole convoluted mistaken identity scenario was the work of the original Green Goblin, who was not dead after all. Ben died heroically battling the Goblin, and the status quo was restored.

But there was still a feeling that Spider-Man had become too complicated, or that it had strayed too far from its roots in Lee and Ditko's tales of the orphaned high school boy. Two attempts to address the problem were writer Kurt Busiek's Untold Tales of Spider-Man (1995 to 1997), set during the Lee-Ditko period, and writer/artist John Byrne's Spider-Man: Chapter One (1998 to 1999), a somewhat revised retelling of Lee and Ditko's original stories.

Finally, Marvel executive Bill Jemas, writer Brian Michael Bendis, and artist Mark Bagley co-created Ultimate Spider-Man in 2000. This was an alternate version of the Spider-Man saga, built on the premise that Peter Parker became Spider-Man at the dawn of the twenty-first century. So here was a Peter who was still a high school student, encountering his classic villains for the first time.

Meanwhile, in the original Spider-Man continuity, the adult Peter has become a high school teacher, whose life has been chronicled by such writers as J. Michael Straczynski and Paul Jenkins.

Ultimate Spider-Man is hardly the first variation on Stan Lee and Steve Ditko's original character. Over the years there have been several female counterparts known as "Spider-Woman." Tom DeFalco co-created the "Spider-Girl" series, portraying the teenage daughter of the middle-aged Peter Parker of an alternate future. Writer Peter David co-created Spider-Man 2099, the Spider-Man of an alternate future, who gained his powers through genetic engineering and could create webbing from his own body. In these aspects, David anticipated the changes that Sam Raimi and his writers made to the Spider-Man story for their feature films.

OPPOSITE: A TWENTY-FIRST-CENTURY PETER PARKER AS DEPICTED IN ULTIMATE SPIDER-MAN.

LEFT: MANY CLASSIC SPIDER-MAN TALES, INCLUDING THE STORY OF UNCLE BEN'S DEATH, WERE RETOLD IN ULTIMATE SPIDER-MAN.

Widely regarded as the best Super Hero movies to date, Sam Raimi's *Spider-Man* and *Spider-Man 2* have brought Marvel's flagship hero to a new height of popularity. Genetic engineering has replaced atomic radiation as the source of the cinematic Spider-Man's powers: Raimi's Peter Parker, played by Tobey Maguire, was a high school senior who was bitten by a genetically altered spider. Raimi made Mary Jane, played by Kirsten Dunst, Peter's love interest from the beginning. Despite the changes that Raimi made in Spider-Man continuity, these two movies were remarkably faithful to the spirit of Stan Lee's 1960s classics. The Green Goblin (played by Willem Dafoe), Doctor Octopus (played by Alfred Molina), Uncle Ben and Aunt May, Harry and Flash, and Jonah and Betty have all turned up so far, and Raimi is preparing a third Spider-Man movie slated for release in 2007.

Appropriately, Stan Lee appeared onscreen briefly in both Spider-Man movies, in acknowledgement of his role in co-creating the character. Lee can take justifiable pride that the teenage hero, the eternal underdog, whom he and Steve Ditko devised for the last issue of a doomed comic book over forty years ago has defied the odds to become one of the leading icons of American pop culture in the twenty-first century.

IND.
12¢
THE INCREDIBLE
HULK
APPROVED BY THE COMICS CODE AUTHORITY
MC
1
MAY
THE STRANGEST MAN OF ALL TIME!!
IS HE MAN OR MONSTER ? OR...
IS HE BOTH
FANTASY AS YOU LIKE IT!

THE INCREDIBLE HULK

THE ORIGINAL ANTIHERO

After Spider-Man, the best-known Marvel Super Hero is not a hero at all, not in conventional terms. Instead he is an antihero, a monster who embodies not our highest ideals but our darker impulses, the personification of rage and violence. Yet despite that, this character retains our sympathies as a lone individual searching for peace and freedom in a cruel and hostile world. He is Dr. Bruce Banner, the brilliant scientist who turned himself into the creature called the "Incredible Hulk."

This is not the kind of character who would have been created in comics' Golden Age of the 1940s. The 1950s waning of public enthusiasm for Super Heroes caused comics companies, including Marvel, to turn to other genres. At the beginning of the 1960s Marvel Comics was pursuing a new trend: science fiction adventures pitting human beings against gigantic monsters. Marvel writer/editor Stan Lee and artist Jack Kirby together concocted such creatures as "Fin Fang Foom" and "Googam, Son of Goom."

Hence, in 1961 when Lee and Kirby experimented with co-creating a new Super Hero team, the Fantastic Four, it made commercial sense that the new comic's first cover featured the heroes battling a gargantuan monster from underground.

What must have surprised readers of the time was that one of the new heroes was himself a monster. Ben Grimm had been transformed by cosmic radiation into the "Thing," a superhumanly strong creature with an orange, rock-like hide. The Thing's monstrous appearance was the visual counterpart to Grimm's violent

OPPOSITE: ISSUE #1 OF THE INCREDIBLE HULK INTRODUCED A CHARACTER MORE AKIN TO THE MONSTERS THAT INHABITED MARVEL COMIC BOOKS IN THE LATE 1950S THAN THE SUPER HEROES OF THE GOLDEN AGE.

temper, as if the beast within Ben Grimm was now manifest to the world. But the Thing was also a tragic figure, and this too was new for Super Hero comics. Ordinary people were frightened and repelled by the Thing. Ben Grimm felt alone and unloved, alienated from the rest of the human race. Nonetheless, despite his occasional fits of temper, Grimm worked alongside his friends in the Fantastic Four, combating menaces to the public, and the world regarded him and his partners as heroes.

With their next new Super Hero series, Lee and Kirby took the alienation concept still further. The title character of the Incredible Hulk, whose first issue was dated May 1962, was another man turned into a monster. But while the Thing was hailed by the public as a hero, the Hulk was an outcast, hunted by the United States military as a threat to national security. The Hulk was the first antihero of modern comics.

Stan Lee has freely admitted that his inspirations for the Hulk were twofold. One was Robert Louis Stevenson's *Dr. Jekyll and Mr. Hyde*, the story of a scientist who transforms himself into the embodiment of the dark, evil side of his own personality. The other was Frankenstein as portrayed by Boris Karloff in the Universal Pictures horror movies of the 1930s: a creature of low intelligence and a highly limited vocabulary who was easily enraged, powerful, and dangerous, and yet at the same time a sympathetic figure, hunted and tormented by those who feared him.

Created in 1962, Hulk was another Cold War product. The origins of nearly all Marvel's classic heroes of the 1960s, including the Fantastic Four and Spider-Man, involved America's fear of radiation. Lee and Kirby also co-created a team of mutants, the X-Men. It is the

BELOW: DR. BRUCE BANNER'S GAMMA-BOMB TEST REFLECTED AMERICAN COLD WAR PREOCCUPATIONS.

OPPOSITE: THE FIRST PAGE OF THE *INCREDIBLE HULK* #1 RIGHTLY PREDICTED THAT HULK WOULD BECOME ONE OF MARVEL'S GREATEST CHARACTERS.

THE HULK
BY— STAN LEE & J. KIRBY
HALF-MAN, HALF-MONSTER, THE MIGHTY HULK THUNDERS OUT OF THE NIGHT TO TAKE HIS PLACE AMONG THE MOST AMAZING CHARACTERS OF ALL TIME!
PART 1
"THE COMING OF THE HULK"
V-709 1

origin of the Hulk, however, that most directly reflects the threat of nuclear Armageddon.

In the first issue of the Incredible Hulk, Dr. Bruce Banner, America's leading nuclear physicist, was supervising the test of his new invention, the gamma bomb, at a military base in the southwestern United States. The gamma bomb had tremendous explosive force, but it was also what we now call a "dirty" bomb, releasing lethal radiation. Lee and Kirby did not invent the concept of "gamma radiation": it is an actual part of the electromagnetic spectrum, and is particularly deadly to living beings.

In 1962 the United States and the Soviet Union had not yet signed the Test Ban Treaty, which permits only underground nuclear tests, and tests of new atomic weapons in desolate areas were regular occurrences. Whether Lee and Kirby intended this or not, a later Hulk writer/artist, John Byrne, has pointed out that, if you look carefully, the gamma bomb test in *Incredible Hulk* #1 was an underground test, and hence the origin story has not grown dated.

It was not explicitly clear in this first story what Lee and Kirby thought of the moral implications of Dr. Banner's creation of this weapon of mass destruction, although the fate that Banner suffered might be regarded as poetic justice.

In any case, Dr. Bruce Banner, as he appeared at the opening of *Incredible Hulk* #1, looked the part of the stereotypical 1950s scientist: bespectaled and wearing a white lab coat, intensely devoted to his work. Banner was clearly in control of his experiment, but his quiet management style did not impress the head of the military base, General "Thunderbolt" Ross. Loud, blustering, and self-important, General Ross was nearly a caricature of military machismo. In Ross's mind, science was

BELOW: THE VERBAL ASSAULTS DR. BANNER ENDURED FROM GENERAL ROSS WERE EASED BY BETTY ROSS'S KINDNESS.

OPPOSITE: BRUCE BANNER WAS WRONG TO TRUST HIS ASSISTANT, IGOR, WHO TURNED OUT TO BE AN ENEMY AGENT.

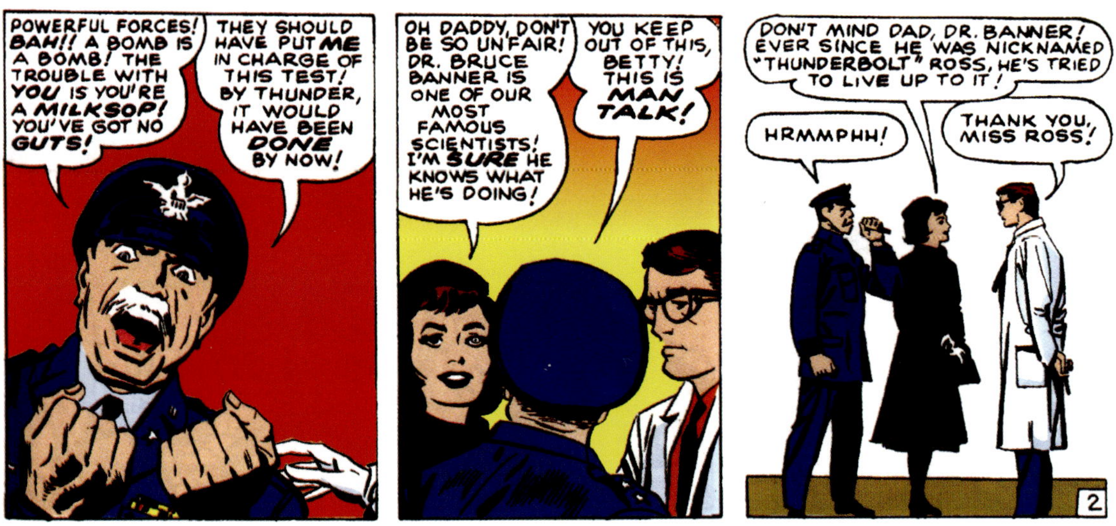

not a fit profession for "real" men, and he constantly berated Banner as a "milksop." Banner simply carried on his work, ignoring the General's chest-thumping as best he could.

Someone who did not share the General's low opinion of Dr. Banner was Ross's own daughter, Betty. Kirby dressed her in an early 1960s suit and pillbox hat, and Lee depicted her as quiet and introverted. As portrayed here, Betty was an archetypal early-1960s action movie heroine, back before the rise of feminism. From today's perspective, readers might wonder why an adult woman was still unemployed and living with her father. More recent Hulk writers, notably Jeph Loeb, have made it clear that Betty's unassertive personality in these early days was the result of living with her domineering, widowed father, who still thought of her as a child.

From the start it was clear that Banner and Betty were strongly attracted to each other, a fact that probably helped motivate the possessive General's anger toward him. But, as was typical of Stan Lee's heroes and heroines in the 1960s, Banner and Betty seemed too introverted, even repressed, to openly acknowledge their feelings to one another.

The countdown to the detonation of the gamma bomb was proceeding smoothly when Dr. Banner suddenly discovered that a teenage boy had driven onto the test site. This was Rick Jones, Lee and Kirby's variation on the standard comic book kid sidekick. Rick's hair style, his use of slang from the late 1950s and early 1960s, his mode of dress, his love of old jalopies, and his general antiestablishment demeanor all marked him as the latest in the line of teenage antiheroes inspired by the late actor James Dean's performance in *Rebel Without a Cause*. In a typical nose-thumbing gesture toward socially approved behavior, Rick had driven out on the test site on a dare, unaware that the bomb was about to go off.

Until he discovered Rick, Dr. Banner was impassively wrapped up in his experiment. But now the same man who had devised a means of killing millions of people could not bring himself to allow a single individual to die. As if his own humanity had been awakened, Banner suddenly turned emotional. He ordered his assistant to halt the countdown while he went to save the boy.

But Lee and Kirby had devised a plot twist that also reflected Cold War paranoia. Banner's assistant has been called by various names over the decades, but the one by which he is best known is Igor Drenkov, an enemy agent presumably in the employ of the Soviets. Drenkov saw this new turn of events as his opportunity to eliminate the West's most brilliant nuclear scientist. Drenkov allowed the countdown to proceed.

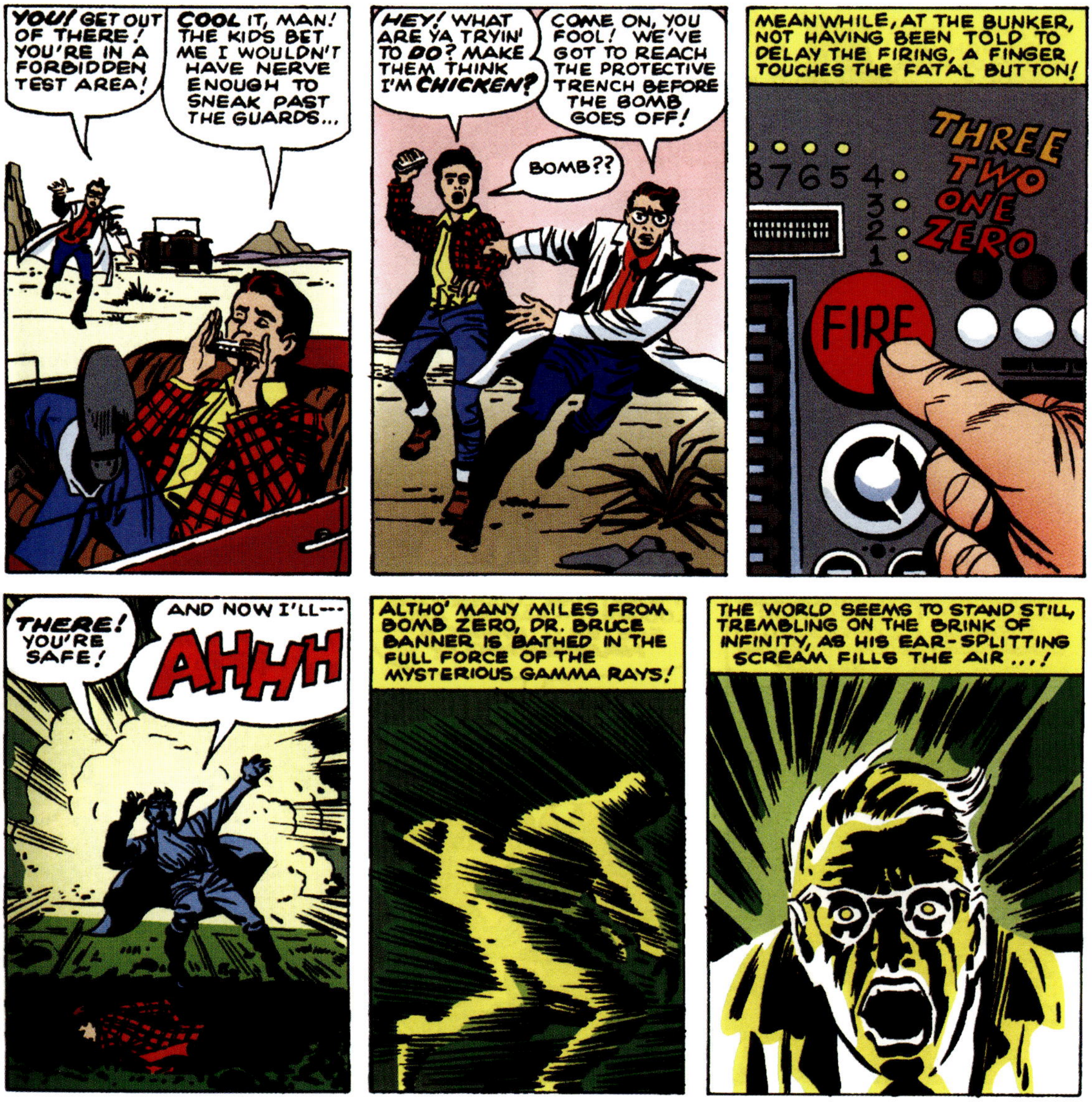

Banner raced onto the testing site and found Rick sitting back in his old car, nonchalantly playing a harmonica. Telling the boy he was in great danger, Banner hurriedly brought him to a trench that would shield them from radiation and pushed the boy in. But before Banner could join him, the bomb went off.

In keeping with Byrne's thesis that the gamma bomb was actually underground, Banner was not obliterated by the blast. But the intense gamma energy broke through to the surface, irradiating Banner.

Yet, astonishingly, Banner did not die. He awoke to find himself brought to safety by the grateful Rick Jones, who was completely unharmed. Jones considered it a miracle that Banner too had survived without any apparent ill effects. As later writers would explain, there was some factor in Banner's genetic makeup that kept the gamma rays from killing him, but they would have a different, perhaps far worse effect.

At sunset, as the horrified Rick watched, Banner began to transform. He grew taller and hundreds of pounds heavier, his facial features turned apelike and unrecognizable, and his personality was similarly warped.

Rick Jones's kind, intellectual benefactor had turned into a brutish and menacing monster. The creature stormed out into the night, where he was soon sighted by soldiers. One of them referred to the massive monster as a "hulk," and the name stuck. (In one of their earlier monster stories, Lee and Kirby had used the name "Hulk" for an alien menace who later battled the new Hulk as "Xemnu the Titan.")

Initially the Hulk's skin was not its familiar green color, but gray. By one account the gray color was a printer's error; by another, Lee intended the Hulk to be gray but then decided with issue #2 that green would look and print better. In subsequent reprintings and retellings of his origin tale, the Hulk was colored green from the start. The gray coloring in issue #1 was universally regarded as a mistake.

However, later generations of writers and readers have had the tendency to regard Stan Lee and Jack Kirby's 1960s Marvel stories as if they were holy scripture. It was John Byrne who established in the

OPPOSITE: IN HIS EFFORT TO SAVE ILL-FATED TEENAGER RICK JONES, BANNER WAS EXPOSED TO THE FULL FORCE OF THE GAMMA-BOMB'S RADIATION.

BELOW: WHEN BANNER FIRST CHANGED INTO THE HULK, HIS SKIN WAS GRAY, BUT BY ISSUE #2 HULK HAD TURNED HIS FAMILIAR GREEN.

1980s that the Hulk really was gray when he first appeared, and subsequent Hulk writers have followed Byrne's lead.

That first night the Hulk marauded through the countryside, and General Ross was determined to stop the creature. But at daybreak the Hulk reverted to the form and personality of Bruce Banner once again, like a werewolf regaining his humanity at dawn. Jeph Loeb has compared Banner's post-Hulk condition to that of an alcoholic awakening after suffering a blackout. Banner was horrified by what he had become. Luckily for him, only Rick Jones knew the secret of his dual identity. Bruce Banner had saved his life, so now Rick Jones would do all he could to help Banner in his struggle against this atomic age curse.

It was as if Bruce Banner had been transformed into the nuclear weapon he had created. The Hulk was like a living incarnation of the power of the gamma bomb. He not only represented the dark side of Bruce Banner's personality, but humanity's potential for destruction.

Banner established a secret laboratory out in the desert, and toward nightfall he would go there with Rick and lock himself behind a thick metal door. Jones would wait there at night, listening to the enraged Hulk pound furiously at the other side of the door. The Hulk was Banner's repressed inner demon, always threatening to escape.

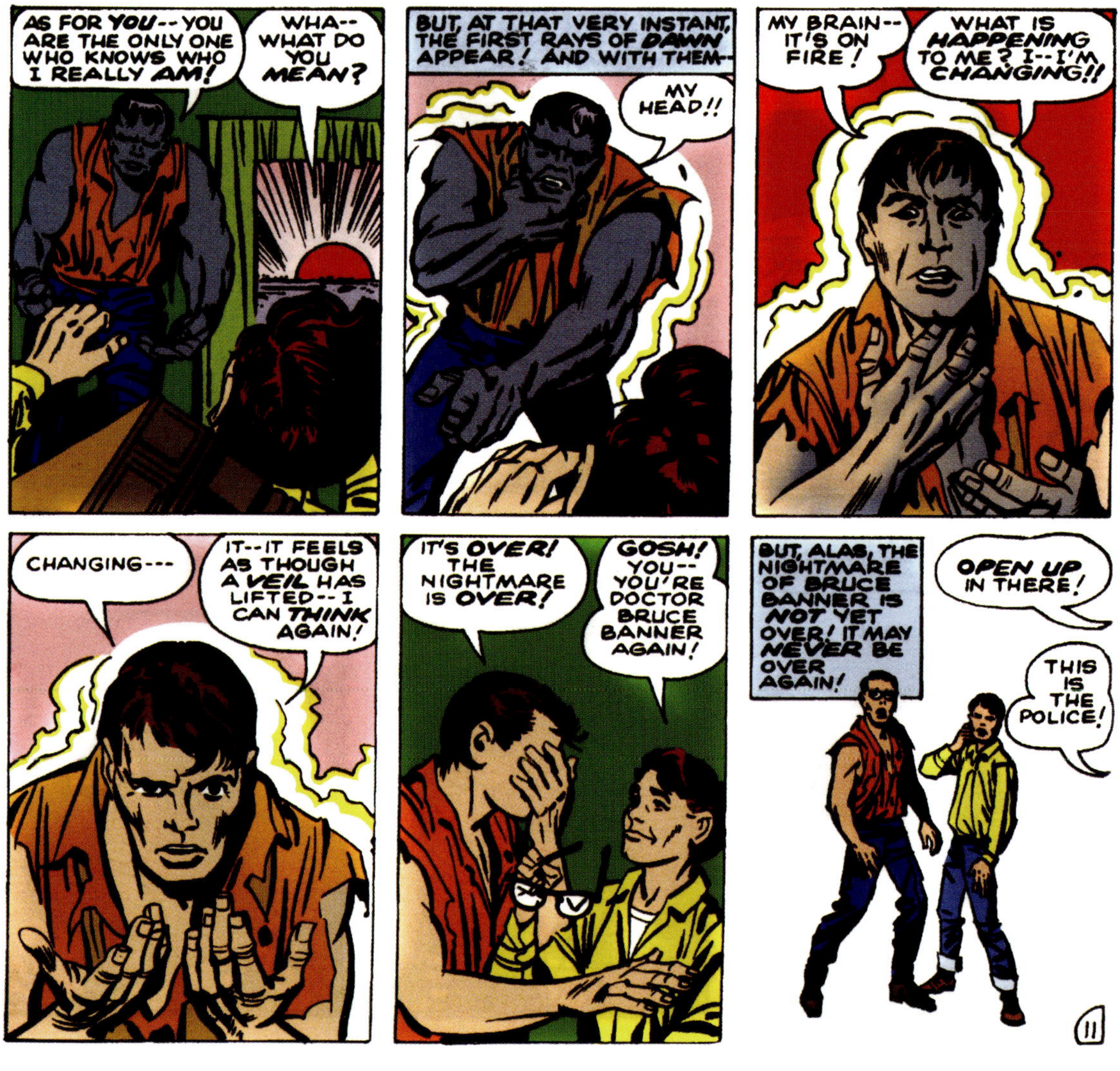

These earliest stories adhered closely to the Cold War and science fiction themes of the time. In the very first issue, the Hulk's secret was discovered by a Soviet scientist known as the "Gargoyle." Even in this initial story, Lee and Kirby created a counterpart to their new antihero: radiation had turned this scientist into a genius, but had mutated him into a physical freak. Captured by the Gargoyle, Banner took pity on his counterpart and devised a means of undoing the radiation's effects, returning him to normalcy. Thus the Soviet scientist found the redemption that eluded Banner and set his benefactor free.

In issue #2 Lee and Kirby pitted the Hulk against a full-scale invasion from outer space, like those in the science fiction stories that were popular in the "B" movies and comics of the time. Against "The Terror of the Toad Men," the Hulk, though a monster, ended up as an unlikely representative of humanity's potential to fight back against oppression and attack. Hence, the Hulk was already becoming more than simply a monster to be feared.

Other aliens and Communists turned up as villains in these early issues, but with issue #3 Lee and Kirby introduced their first costumed super-villain into the series: the "Ringmaster," with his "Circus of Crime," was a reworking of a villain Kirby had co-created for Captain America Comics in the 1940s.

For issue #5 Lee and Kirby co-created one of the Hulk's leading foes, "Tyrannus," the last emperor of ancient Rome, who had discovered an underground fountain of youth that had sustained his life for centuries. Now he ruled an underground kingdom of creatures called "Subterraneans" and dreamed of conquering the surface world.

What made Tyrannus a perfect villain for the Hulk was the contrast between them. Tyrannus was handsome, elegant, brilliantly intelligent, and as the last ruler of the Roman Empire, the embodiment of civilization: all things

OPPOSITE: BRUCE BANNER HAD NO IDEA WHAT HAD HAPPENED TO HIM DURING HIS FIRST NIGHT AS THE HULK.

ABOVE: IN ISSUE #2 HULK FOUGHT OFF THE TOAD MEN AND GAVE READERS THEIR FIRST GLIMPSE OF HIS HEROIC SIDE.

BELOW: GARGOYLE LEARNED ABOUT THE HULK IN ISSUE #1 AND SET OUT TO CAPTURE HIM.

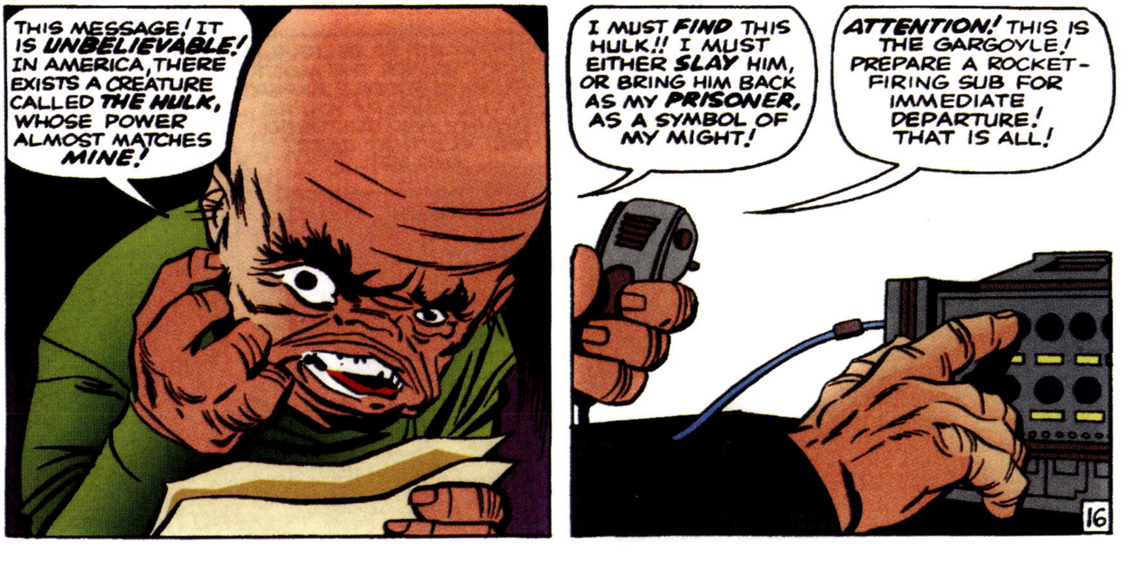

THE INCREDIBLE HULK
"Beauty AND THE BEAST!"
SCRIPT: STAN LEE • ART: JACK KIRBY
INKING: DICK AYERS • LETTERING: ART SIMEK
TYRANNUS
MISS BETTY ROSS
THE INCREDIBLE HULK
X-48
1

the Hulk was not. On the other hand, the Hulk was primal, like a caveman before the rise of civilization. Enemies like Tyrannus chose to menace and even enslave other people; the Hulk often only fought back against those who attacked him. Tyrannus represented the evils of civilization; the Hulk embodied the natural freedom of the individual.

Lee titled this story "Beauty and the Beast," since he and Kirby were introducing this old fairy tale theme into the Hulk series. Tyrannus took Betty Ross hostage to prevent General Ross from opposing him. It was the Hulk who rescued Betty, like King Kong saving Fay Wray's character from dinosaurs in the 1933 film, though Betty had no idea that this fearsome creature was the man she loved.

In the initial Hulk series, Lee and Kirby kept experimenting with the character. The Hulk became more intelligent and articulate, and hence less like Frankenstein and more like Mr. Hyde. Though arrogant and hot-tempered, this Hulk had self-control and, though not a genius like Banner, was a cunning opponent. His transformations no longer took place at dawn and dusk: instead he used a machine that projected gamma radiation, allowing him to change between his two personas.

Issue #6 was not drawn by Kirby but by Lee's collaborator on Amazing Spider-Man, Steve Ditko. This story, which pitted the Hulk against an alien called the "Metal Master," treated him more like a conventional Super Hero. The Hulk actually used trickery to thwart the Metal Master's attempt to conquer the Earth, and the grateful United States government awarded the Hulk a pardon for the destruction he had perpetrated in the past.

Where would the Hulk go from here? Unfortunately, issue #6 (March 1963) was the last in the Hulk's original series: the Incredible Hulk was canceled due to poor sales.

OPPOSITE: THE "BEAUTY AND THE BEAST" STORY INTRODUCED HULK'S FIRST GREAT NEMESIS, TYRANNUS.

ABOVE: HULK WAS MORE HERO THAN MONSTER WHEN HE DEFEATED THE METAL MASTER IN ISSUE #6.

BELOW: HULK FELT HE WAS UNDER-APPRECIATED WHEN THE GOVERNMENT PARDONED HIM AS A REWARD FOR DEFEATING THE METAL MASTER.

Still, Lee and Kirby would not give up on their creation. That same month they put the Hulk in the first issue of their brand new comic book, the Avengers. This series was created to bring together several of the stars of Marvel's growing line of Super Hero comics. In the first issue, "Loki," the Norse god of evil, decided that the Hulk was powerful enough to defeat his nemesis, the thunder god Thor. Hence, Loki used magic to wreck a train, making it look as if the Hulk had been responsible. Loki assumed that Thor would go in pursuit of the Hulk, but three other new Super Heroes—Iron Man, Ant-Man and the Wasp—showed up as well. The heroes battled the Hulk, but soon Loki's guilt was revealed, and Thor captured his evil foster brother. Ant-Man and the Wasp suggested that the heroes band together as a team. The Avengers, and the Hulk, despite being a loner by temperament, went along with the idea.

But the Hulk did not stay for long. In the very next issue, a shapeshifting alien called the "Space Phantom" impersonated the Hulk in order to attack

BELOW: AFTER THE HULK SERIES WAS CANCELLED, HULK BRIEFLY COLLABORATED WITH THE AVENGERS UNTIL A MISUNDERSTANDING DROVE HIM INTO SOLITUDE ONCE AGAIN.

OPPOSITE: (TOP) HULK TURNED UP IN THE AMAZING SPIDER-MAN; (BOTTOM) HE ALSO WENT TOE-TO-TOE WITH THE THING IN A BATTLE OF MARVEL MONSTERS.

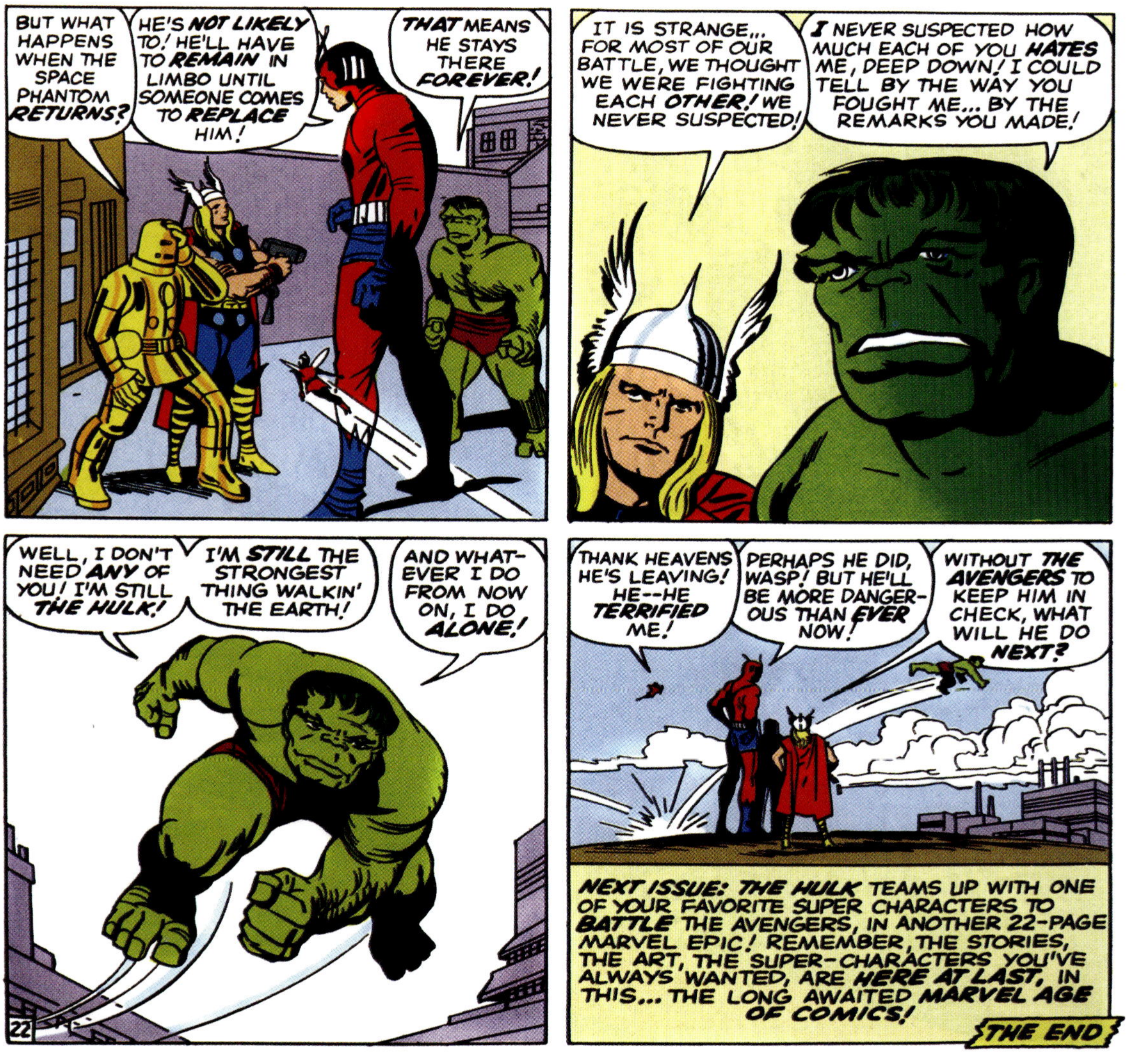

the Avengers. In retaliation, the other Avengers battled the real Hulk. Once again, the actual enemy's trickery was exposed, but the Hulk realized how much the other Avengers distrusted him. Embittered, the Hulk quit the team. (Two issues later, Captain America would take over the Hulk's spot with the Avengers.)

Having abandoned the experiment of treating the Hulk more as a conventional Super Hero, now Lee and Kirby portrayed him as an outright menace. The Hulk battled his former allies in *Avengers* #3 and #5, and both the Avengers and the Fantastic Four in *Fantastic Four* #25 and #26. Though they had earlier fought briefly in *Fantastic Four* #12, this two-part book was the first great battle between the Hulk and the Thing; such similar characters proved to be natural opponents. The Hulk even attacked Spider-Man when the latter inadvertently disturbed him in his desert lair in *Amazing Spider-Man* #14. In this story, drawn by Ditko, the Hulk was reverting to the savage creature of his origin tale.

Finally, Stan Lee gave the Hulk his own series again, this time as the second feature of Tales to Astonish, starting with issue #60 (October 1964). Tales to Astonish was one of Marvel's "split" books, divided between two series. Steve Ditko collaborated with Lee on the first eight installments of the Hulk's series in Astonish, and it was here that the classic version of the Hulk achieved his definitive form.

Now Bruce Banner transformed into the Hulk whenever his heartbeat rose above a certain level, whether due to anger, tension, or fear. Similarly, if the Hulk's anger subsided and he grew peaceful enough, he would revert to Banner.

The Hulk's intellect was severely limited, as was his vocabulary: he characteristically substituted his name, Hulk, for the pronoun "I." But the Hulk was not dim-witted; rather, Banner's intellect and personality had regressed to those of a rather bad-tempered child. The danger lay in the fact that this "child" had the body of a superhumanly powerful adult and was capable of shattering mountains.

The Hulk sought solitude and peace, but neither the military nor his various enemies would grant him his wish. Hence, the Hulk usually fought only in response to being attacked.

RIGHT: GENERAL ROSS USED THE FULL FORCE OF THE MILITARY TO PURSUE HULK, WHO WANTED ONLY TO BE LEFT ALONE.

OPPOSITE: (TOP) LABORER SAM STERNS WAS EXPOSED TO GAMMA RADIATION WHILE WORKING AT A CHEMICAL RESEARCH PLANT; (BOTTOM) THE RADIATION GAVE STERNS SUPERHUMAN INTELLIGENCE, AND HE BECAME THE VILLAINOUS LEADER.

Though the Hulk claimed he only wanted to be left alone, he actually longed for friendship and love. Unless he was seized by blind rage, the Hulk welcomed the companionship of Rick Jones. Lee and Kirby turned Jones into the Avengers' sidekick, but Rick has continued to appear as a supporting character in the Incredible Hulk off and on over the decades. More importantly, the Hulk felt affection for Betty Ross and sought to protect her.

General "Thunderbolt" Ross, on the other hand, became the Hulk's implacable enemy. Ross's obsession with capturing or destroying the Hulk has rivaled that of Captain Ahab for Moby Dick. Of course, the Hulk bitterly hates General Ross as well. Thus there is a weird Freudian triangle at the heart of the Incredible Hulk, with an aged father figure (Ross) locked in combat with a powerful younger man (Hulk), and a woman (Betty, Ross's daughter and Banner's girlfriend) caught between them.

The one person that the Hulk has hated more than General Ross is Bruce Banner himself. The split in Banner's personality runs so deeply that the Hulk does not intellectually grasp the fact that he and Banner are one and the same. But the Hulk knows that "weak, puny" Banner is his enemy, who somehow casts him into oblivion every so often.

As for Banner, he only dimly remembers his actions as the Hulk. Banner continually finds himself waking up in places with little idea of how he got there or what happened. Banner's long, mysterious absences (due to the Hulk's actions) increased General Ross's hostility towards him. In response, the General brought in security expert Major Glenn Talbot (debuting in *Tales to Astonish* #61), who not only became Banner's nemesis, but also his rival for Betty's affections. Betty, however, remained devoted to Banner despite the turmoil the Hulk brought to their lives.

In a combination of machismo and childishness, the Hulk boasted that he was "the strongest one that lives," and he was probably right. The Hulk was larger and stronger than Spider-Man or the Thing, and was at least a match for Marvel's strongest hero, Thor. Moreover, it was eventually established that the angrier the Hulk got, the stronger he became. To this day there is no known upper limit to the Hulk's strength.

Though not absolutely invulnerable, the Hulk's thick, massive body is not only bulletproof, but can also withstand the impact of any conventional weaponry. Time and again Hulk readers have seen full-scale military attacks on the lone monster, who has not only survived, but has triumphed, demolishing tanks and downing planes.

While handsomer, more graceful Super Heroes can fly, the Hulk also travels through the air, not by flying but by jumping, like an enormous leapfrog. The Hulk's powerful leg muscles can propel him through the air for miles with a single leap.

It was in *Tales to Astonish* #62 (December 1964) that Lee and Ditko introduced the man who would become the Hulk's leading villain. This criminal mastermind was a variation on the Gargoyle, but this one would never reform. Sam Sterns was a laborer who was not particularly bright until he was exposed to radioactive waste. The gamma radiation mutated Sterns, turning his skin green like the Hulk's, but instead of increasing his strength, it magnified his intelligence to a superhuman level. In fact, both his brain and his skull grew to enormous size. Deciding that he was now superior to ordinary humans, Sterns was determined to become their ruler and hence called himself the "Leader." The war between the Leader's brain and the Hulk's brawn has continued ever since.

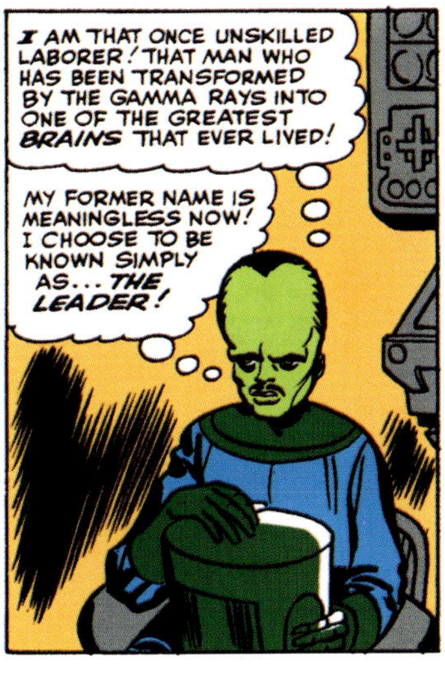

Jack Kirby returned to the Hulk series in *Astonish* #68, remaining through issue #84. During this time Lee and Kirby continued to make a habit of undercutting the conventions of Super Hero stories. Readers might have expected that Banner's secret would never be exposed, but in *Astonish* #77 (March 1966) Glenn Talbot learned that Bruce Banner was the Hulk, and soon the entire world knew. Now Bruce Banner would lead the life of a fugitive, wandering the world, trying to escape the authorities hunting him.

Among Jack Kirby's successors as artist on the Hulk series was Gil Kane, a new recruit to Marvel. Together Lee and Kane created the Hulk's second-most notorious recurring villain in *Tales to Astonish* #90 (April 1967). Like Igor Drenkov, he was another Communist spy who

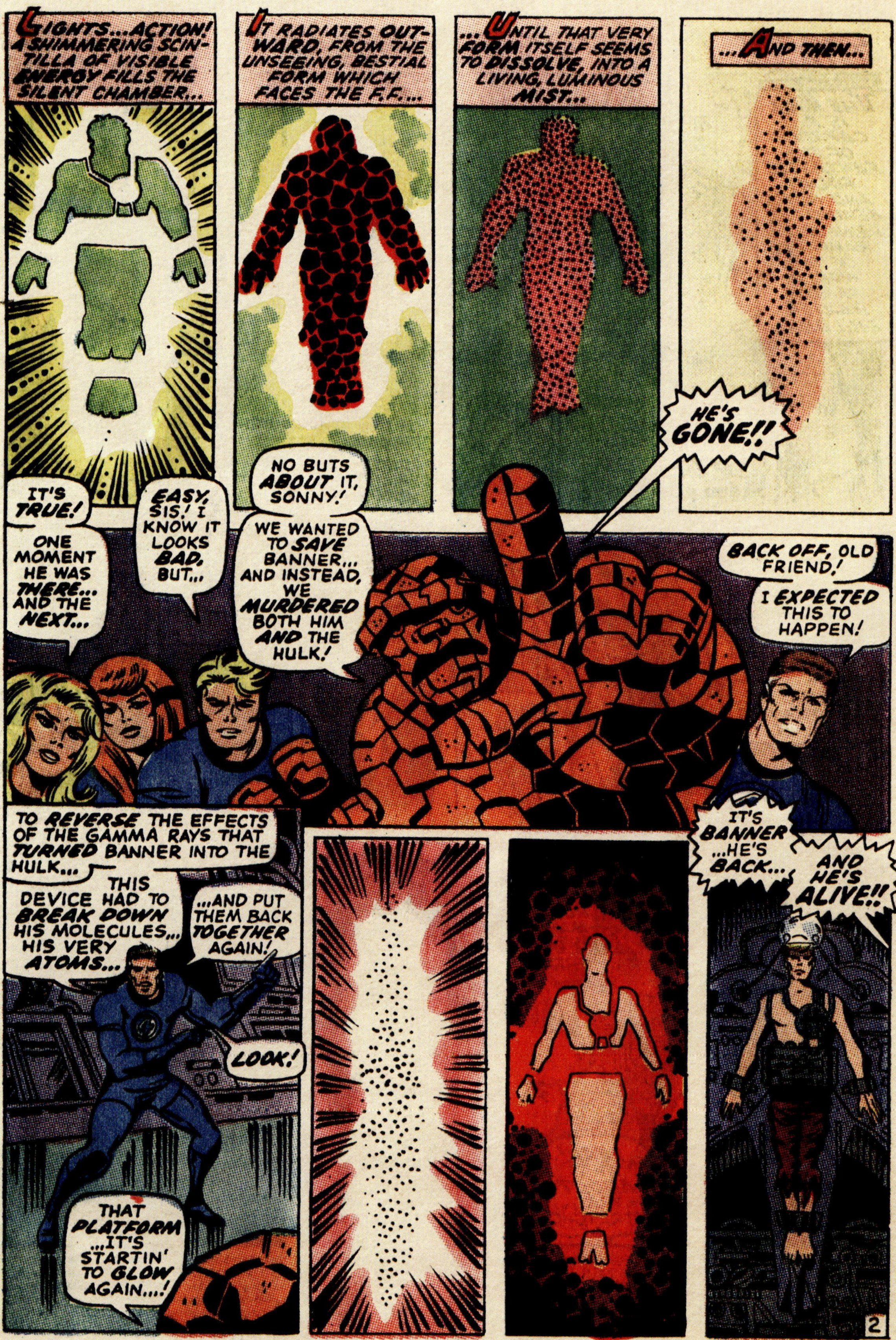
LIGHTS...ACTION! A SHIMMERING SCINTILLA OF VISIBLE ENERGY FILLS THE SILENT CHAMBER...
IT RADIATES OUTWARD, FROM THE UNSEEING, BESTIAL FORM WHICH FACES THE F.F. ...
...UNTIL THAT VERY FORM ITSELF SEEMS TO DISSOLVE, INTO A LIVING, LUMINOUS MIST...
...AND THEN...
HE'S GONE!!
IT'S TRUE!
ONE MOMENT HE WAS THERE... AND THE NEXT...
EASY, SIS! I KNOW IT LOOKS BAD, BUT...
NO BUTS ABOUT IT, SONNY!
WE WANTED TO SAVE BANNER... AND INSTEAD, WE MURDERED BOTH HIM AND THE HULK!
BACK OFF, OLD FRIEND!
I EXPECTED THIS TO HAPPEN!
TO REVERSE THE EFFECTS OF THE GAMMA RAYS THAT TURNED BANNER INTO THE HULK...
THIS DEVICE HAD TO BREAK DOWN HIS MOLECULES... HIS VERY ATOMS...
...AND PUT THEM BACK TOGETHER AGAIN!
LOOK!
THAT PLATFORM ...IT'S STARTIN' TO GLOW AGAIN...!
IT'S BANNER ...HE'S BACK...
AND HE'S ALIVE!!

OPPOSITE: BRUCE BANNER WAS FINALLY ABLE TO GET RID OF HIS HULK ALTEREGO WITH THE HELP OF THE FANTASTIC FOUR'S REED RICHARDS.

LEFT: NO LONGER ISOLATED BY HIS LIFE AS THE HULK, BANNER FINALLY ASKED FOR BETTY'S HAND IN MARRIAGE.

had infiltrated General Ross's base, this time as a soldier. Discovering a gamma ray generator that Banner had invented, the spy turned it on himself, hoping to gain superhuman powers. Indeed he did, as the radiation mutated him into another green-skinned, super-strong monster. In this case, the spy retained his original intelligence and personality, but his reptilian features made him far more grotesque than the humanoid Hulk. Aghast, Betty Ross called this new monster an "Abomination," the name he retains today. By abducting Betty, the Abomination earned the wrath of the Hulk, and their feud has continued for decades.

With Marvel's growing success and changes in its distribution system, the company was able to begin expanding its line of comics. The Sub-Mariner, who shared Tales to Astonish, was spun off into his own monthly title, and so with issue #101 (April 1968), Tales to Astonish was renamed The Incredible Hulk. After his abrupt six-issue run at the decade's start, the Hulk was once again the star of his own comic book. With issue #108 (October 1966), a new creative team settled in for a long run: writer/editor Stan Lee and artist Herb Trimpe. Even after Lee left (with issue #120), Trimpe continued to draw the Hulk into the mid-1970s, and Hulk remains Trimpe's signature character to this day.

Roy Thomas succeeded Stan Lee as the Hulk's writer and made major contributions to the character's story. In issue #123 (January 1970) Thomas had Reed Richards, leader of the Fantastic Four, succeed in curing Banner, who quickly proposed to the long-suffering Betty. But in the next issue their wedding ceremony was interrupted by the Leader, who irradiated Banner, causing him to transform back into a savage Hulk.

One of the important landmarks in the Hulk's history is issue #140 (June 1971), plotted by the acclaimed author Harlan Ellison, a lifelong comics aficionado, and dialogued by Thomas. In this classic story, a villain has turned a shrinking ray on the Hulk, dispatching him into a "microverse," where he ends up on a planet inhabited by a race of green-skinned humanoids. There, sorcerers used their magic to enable Bruce Banner's intellect and personality to take control of the Hulk's body. As a result the Hulk became a true hero, the champion of the green-skinned people, whose beautiful princess, "Jarella," fell in love with him. It appeared that the Hulk had found an earthly paradise, and, once again, he was on the brink of marriage when fate intervened. The Hulk abruptly grew bigger and was transported back to Earth, where he once again became a monster with the mind of a child.

For the following issue, #141 (July 1971), Thomas and Trimpe created another long-running member of the Hulk's supporting cast, psychiatrist Dr. Leonard Samson. Yet another victim of exposure to gamma radiation, Dr. Samson gained superhuman strength but retained his normal skin color; instead, his hair grew long and green. Now he became known as "Doc Samson." (Thomas was alluding not only to the biblical Samson but also to the

OPPOSITE: IN 1980, THE HULK'S POPULARITY AS A TELEVISION CHARACTER INSPIRED STAN LEE AND JOHN BUSCEMA TO INVENT THE SAVAGE SHE-HULK.

ABOVE: ALTHOUGH THE ORIGINAL SHE-HULK BOOK WAS UNSUCCESSFUL, JOHN BYRNE CREATED A COMEDY SERIES FOR THE CHARACTER IN 1989.

1930s pulp novel character "Doc Savage," a forerunner to today's Super Heroes.) Not only was Doc Samson a Super Hero who could hold his own in combat with the Hulk, but in later years he also became Bruce Banner's psychiatrist. As the series explored Banner's psychology in greater depth, Samson's role grew more significant.

The Hulk had not worked out as a founding member of the Avengers, but Roy Thomas put him on the original roster of his new Super Hero group, the "Defenders," who debuted in *Marvel Feature* #1 (December 1971) and won their own title soon afterwards (August 1972). The Defenders were described as a "non-team team," a loosely knit alliance, whose other founding members included the Sub-Mariner and the sorcerer "Doctor Strange," whose spells could restrain the Hulk when he became overly tempermental. The Defenders have appeared, off and on, for over three decades, with the Hulk serving as a member more often than not.

The Hulk first came to television as one of the five stars of the *Marvel Super Heroes* show in 1966. This series is infamous for its absolute minimal use of animation, but it took its stories directly from the comics and put artwork by Kirby and Ditko onscreen.

The Hulk's fame skyrocketed when he starred in two live-action, made-for-TV movies in the mid-1970s. Their popularity led to the debut of the weekly television series *The Incredible Hulk* in March 1978. In the days before computer-genarated images (CGI), the protagonist was performed by two actors. The late Bill Bixby portrayed the long-suffering Dr. Banner, who was renamed David (allegedly because "Bruce Banner" sounded too much like the typical alliterative comic book name), and the bodybuilder Lou Ferrigno, aided by green body paint, portrayed the Hulk.

The television show avoided the super-villains and spectacular feats that were standard parts of the Hulk comic books, aiming for greater realism (and lower special effects budgets). Instead, the *Incredible Hulk* show was obviously patterned after a previous television hit, *The Fugitive*, which was itself derived from Victor Hugo's classic novel *Les Misérables*. Thought to have been killed by the Hulk, David Banner wandered the country, becoming involved with different people. Inevitably, in the course of each episode, Banner would become the Hulk, tangling with the story's villains. As a result, a persistent newspaper reporter investigating the Hulk kept turning up, and Banner was always forced to move on in order to preserve his secret: that he himself was the Hulk.

To capitalize on the character's popularity on television, Marvel published a full-color magazine, *The Hulk!*, which ran similar stories about Banner's wanderings (but still called him Bruce).

Probably to prevent anyone else from creating a female counterpart to the Hulk, Stan Lee and his frequent collaborator, comics artist John Buscema, co-created their own for Marvel in the *Savage She-Hulk* #1 (February 1980). This issue introduced Bruce Banner's cousin, Jennifer Walters, a somewhat introverted lawyer working as the Los Angeles district attorney. When Jennifer was shot by a criminal, Bruce Banner gave her a transfusion of his own blood. It saved her life, but the combination of Banner's radioactive blood and her genetic similarity to her cousin transformed Jennifer into a raging, super-strong, green-skinned monster.

The She-Hulk's original series was not a success, presumably because she was too much like the original Hulk without establishing a distinctive identity of her own.

This changed thanks to Marvel writer Roger Stern. The idea behind the Hulk was that the gamma rays had unleashed a repressed side of Bruce Banner's personality. So Stern decided that the She-Hulk would embody Jennifer Walters's repressed fantasy of what she wanted to be: tall, beautiful, extroverted, strong, witty, and happy. Stern put this new, glamorous She-Hulk into the Avengers. His friend John Byrne, one of the leading comics writer/artists of his generation, liked Stern's version so much that he made her a substitute member of the Fantastic Four. Ultimately Byrne starred her in a new title, the Sensational She-Hulk (May 1989), a wonderfully imaginative and funny comedy-adventure series. Not only did it lovingly kid the conventions of Super Hero comics, but Byrne had She-Hulk "break the fourth wall," directly addressing the readers and even Byrne himself.

Meanwhile, in the regular Incredible Hulk monthly comic, writers such as Steve Englehart, Len Wein, Roger Stern, and Bill Mantlo had been putting the characters through the sort of soap-operatic storylines that Marvel favored. Jarella had come to Earth, but she died heroically saving a child from a wall that collapsed during one of the Hulk's battles. Betty Ross married Bruce's longtime rival, Glenn Talbot, who grew as obsessive towards Banner's alter ego as General Ross had and finally perished in combat with the Hulk. As for the General himself, his mania led him to commit treason by conspiring with the Abomination against the Hulk. His crime exposed, Ross nearly committed suicide and then vanished.

Bill Mantlo's greatest contribution to the Hulk's legend was the story he wrote for *The Incredible Hulk* #312 (October 1985). Consisting mainly

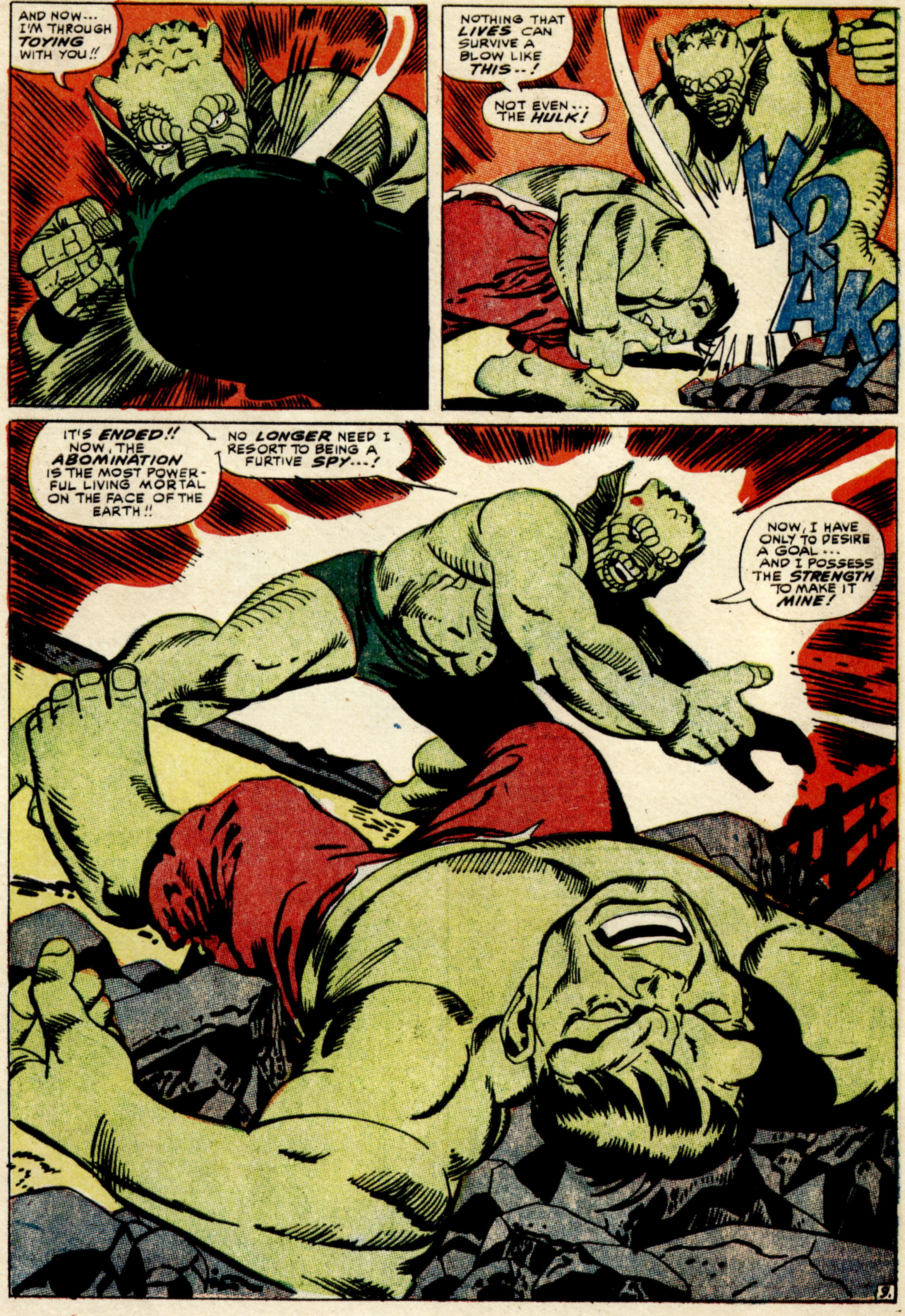
AND NOW... I'M THROUGH TOYING WITH YOU!!
NOTHING THAT LIVES CAN SURVIVE A BLOW LIKE THIS--!
NOT EVEN... THE HULK!
KRAK!
IT'S ENDED!! NOW, THE ABOMINATION IS THE MOST POWERFUL LIVING MORTAL ON THE FACE OF THE EARTH!!
NO LONGER NEED I RESORT TO BEING A FURTIVE SPY...!
NOW, I HAVE ONLY TO DESIRE A GOAL... AND I POSSESS THE STRENGTH TO MAKE IT MINE!

THE HALL OF MIRRORS

Given the dramatic logic of serial fiction, it was inevitable that the longer the Hulk's series ran, the more he would encounter other people who, like himself, had been transformed into superhuman beings by gamma radiation.

Stan Lee and Jack Kirby's original concept for the Hulk was that he was an Atomic Age version of Dr. Jekyll and Mr. Hyde: the scientist who experimented with mysterious forces that released the beast within himself. Whereas the Victorian Henry Jekyll was transformed by a chemical concoction, the Cold War's Bruce Banner was mutated by the gamma radiation from an exploding nuclear bomb.

In the real world, intense gamma radiation will kill a person outright, and in the Marvel Universe it has the same lethal effect on most people. But there are certain individuals on Marvel-earth who, like Bruce Banner, possess a factor in their genetic makeup that not only prevents them from dying from overexposure to gamma radiation but also causes them to mutate.

Usually the skin of these gamma-irradiated individuals turns green. Apart from this color change, each of these genetically unique individuals mutates in a different way. The clearest contrast is between the Hulk and the second gamma-mutated being in the Hulk series, his archenemy the Leader. Dr. Bruce Banner gained seemingly limitless superhuman strength as a result of his mutation into the Hulk, but his genius was dimmed to a toddler's intelligence level. In contrast, Sam Sterns grew no stronger physically as a result of radiation, but his low intelligence in his human form was raised to superhuman heights when he became the Leader.

In fiction, a villain psychologically represents a sinister side of the hero himself. Hence, the Leader could be regarded as symbolizing Hulk's own potential for evil. What if Bruce Banner turned his own great intellect against his fellow man? What if the Hulk used his superhuman powers to try to dominate the "normal" humans? Combine the answers to both questions and you have the Leader.

As the Hulk series evolved, it became clear that the gamma radiation unleashed a repressed side of the personality of the person it mutated. Hence, Sam Sterns, the passively submissive laborer, became the Leader, whose name signaled his intention of ruling the world.

Gamma radiation gave the Abomination strength comparable to the Hulk's, but it did not alter his personality or intelligence whatsoever. Perhaps that is because Emil Blonsky, the enemy spy who became the Abomination, was already a "monster" in moral terms. The radiation instead made his facial features far more inhuman and repulsive than those of the Hulk's, as if his twisted psyche was now pictured on his face. While the Hulk is no threat unless he is provoked, the Abomination is exactly the sort of menace that General "Thunderbolt" Ross claims the Hulk to be.

In an ironic stroke, the Abomination's troubled relationship with his estranged wife Nadia contrasts with the love and loyalty between Banner/Hulk and his wife Betty Ross. Even Betty was temporarily mutated by gamma rays into a savage, monstrous creature, half-woman, half-bird, called the "Harpy" (in *Incredible Hulk* #168, October 1973).

Whereas Banner's "other self" proved to be a monster, gamma radiation enabled the studious Dr. Leonard Samson and Banner's introverted cousin Jennifer Walters to realize their heroic, extroverted potentials as Doc Samson and the She-Hulk.

The ultimate gamma-irradiated villain in the Hulk series is the "Maestro," a version of the Hulk from an alternate future time line. He combines the Abomination's physical might and brutality with the Leader's determination to use his great mind to dominate the human race. Thus the greatest villain in the Hulk series is this nightmare version of Bruce Banner himself.

SPY EMIL BLONSKY WAS TRANSFORMED INTO THE ABOMINATION IN *TALES TO ASTONISH* #90. HIS EQUAL PHYSICAL STRENGTH ESTABLISHED HIM AS THE EVIL FOIL TO BANNER'S HULK PERSONA.

RIGHT: ISSUE #312 FEATURED LANDMARK STORIES THAT GAVE THE READERS GLIMPSES INTO HULK'S PAINFUL PAST.

OPPOSITE: IN THAT ISSUE READERS DISCOVERED THAT AN ABUSIVE FATHER WAS TO BLAME FOR HULK'S SPLIT PERSONALITY.

of flashbacks to Bruce Banner's past, Mantlo's tale established that Banner suffered from what psychiatrists call multiple personality disorder. Mantlo revealed that Bruce's father, Dr. Brian Banner, was physically and verbally abusive towards both his wife and son. In fact, the disturbed Brian Banner finally murdered his wife. Bruce Banner grew up repressing the intense rage he felt toward his father until the gamma bomb radiation gave that rage physical form as the Hulk. Thus the Hulk was the physical manifestation of Bruce Banner's alternate personality, which he had repressed since his childhood.

This was a revolutionary approach to the Hulk, and though Mantlo's story had little impact at first, later Hulk writers, notably Peter David, based their treatment of the character on Mantlo's foundation.

Only two issues after Mantlo's masterpiece, John Byrne took over the Incredible Hulk as writer and artist for what proved to be only a handful of issues. But in that short period of time, Byrne made his own lasting contributions. In Byrne's initial storyline, Banner and the Hulk were split into separate physical beings. Roy Thomas had briefly experimented with this trick in the 1970s. Byrne, however, used the opportunity to hold a new wedding ceremony for Bruce and Betty. As in the Thomas version, the ceremony was interrupted, this time by a vengeful General Ross, nearly insane and dressed in tattered clothes. Ross fired his gun at Banner,

MOMMY!
YOU MAY HAVE FOOLED YOUR MOTHER--
FWAK!
--BUT I'VE KNOWN WHAT YOU WOULD BECOME EVER SINCE THE BEGINNING!
BRUCE! BRIAN, YOU ARE INSANE! HOW COULD YOU HIT OUR CHILD--?!
CHILD? NO NORMAL CHILD, NOT THAT ONE!
HE'S SOMETHING DIFFERENT... INHUMAN!
"MY SON"--THE MONSTER!

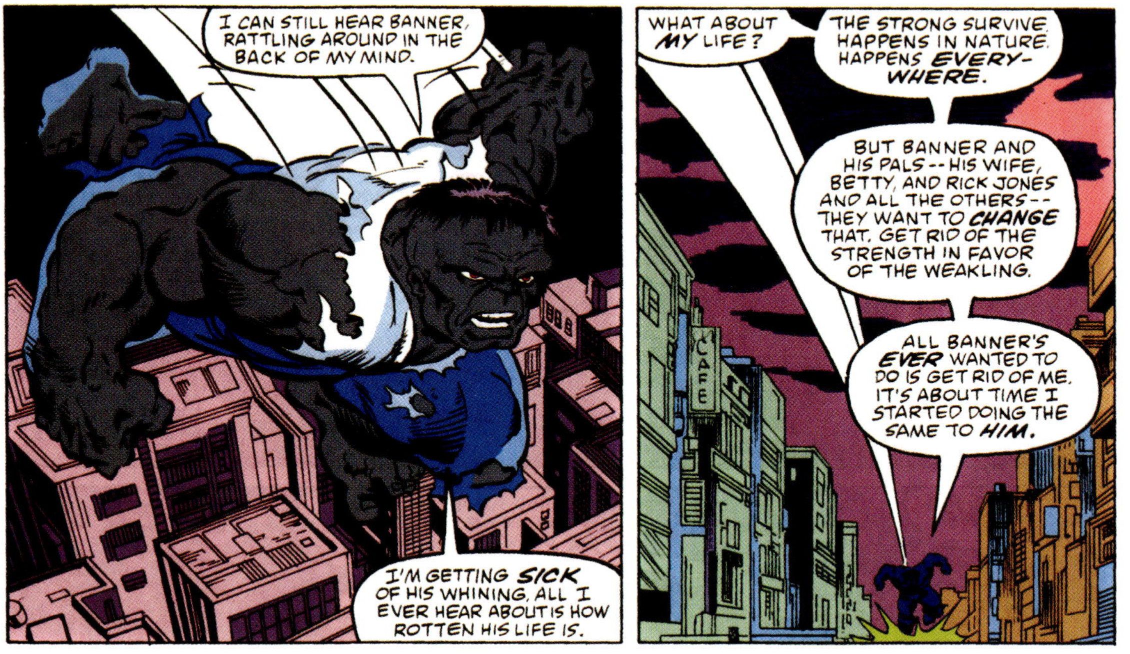

but best man Rick Jones took the bullet, which luckily proved nonlethal. At long last, Bruce Banner and Betty Ross were pronounced man and wife in issue #319 (May 1986).

Before he left the series, Byrne also established that the Hulk of *Incredible Hulk* #1 really had been gray. Taking over the book, writer/artist Al Milgrom followed Byrne's lead: Milgrom fused Banner and his monstrous alter ego back into a single physical being, but the result was not the green Hulk but the original gray Hulk. After (seemingly) killing off General Ross, Milgrom too departed the series.

Now began the often-brilliant, decade-long run of Peter David as the writer of the *Incredible Hulk*. David's distinctive authorial voice breathed new life into a series that had frequently seemed moribund over the years. Whereas his predecessors were often basically imitating Stan Lee's Hulk stories, David gave the series a vivid, contemporary feel. His characteristically sharp, ironic dialogue was not only reliably witty but lent his characters further psychological depth. David had the good fortune to be teamed with exciting new artists, notably Todd McFarlane and Dale Keown. Perhaps best of all, Peter David was continually experimenting with the series, managing to turn the Hulk concept in unexpected new directions while never betraying its past.

For example, David immediately took to the story potential of the new/old gray Hulk, whose cynical, hard-edged adult personality so sharply contrasted with the terrible-toddler persona of the familiar green Hulk. Building on Mantlo's landmark story, David established that the gray Hulk was yet another of Banner's multiple personalities. David astounded readers when he had the gray Hulk briefly disappear and then reemerge wearing a suit, tie, and hat as "Mr. Fixit," an enforcer for an organized crime family in Las Vegas. No longer mentally and emotionally stuck at the level of a small child, this mature Hulk even had a girlfriend, Margo Chandler, who would later end up marrying Rick Jones.

Before readers could tire of any new status quo he devised for the Hulk, Peter David would take the series off in yet another surprising direction. Aided by the hypnotic powers of his old foe the Ringmaster, Doc Samson succeeded in merging the three known personalities of Bruce Banner—Banner the scientist, the gray Hulk, and the green Hulk—into one, supposedly curing his multiple personality disorder once and for all. The result, physically, was a new, handsome green Hulk with Banner's intelligence. Mantlo had tried a similar version of the Hulk, making him a conventional Super Hero. But David kept his intelligent green Hulk an outsider: he joined the "Pantheon," a mysterious organization that combatted evil all over the globe, even if it meant fighting governments—including that of the United States!

Still later, Banner was reunited with Betty, who had briefly become, of all things, a nun, and they resumed married life, trying unsuccessfully to hide from public view. Since classic comics characters rarely stayed dead, David also ended up resurrecting General Ross.

Peter David and artist George Perez collaborated on the mini-series Hulk: Future Imperfect, in which the Hulk journeys into a projected future timeline in which the evil "Maestro"—yet another alternate personality—dominates the world.

OPPOSITE: DURING HIS RUN AS WRITER OF THE INCREDIBLE HULK, PETER DAVID'S SHARP DIALOGUE EXPLORED NEW DEPTHS OF THE HULK'S PSYCHE.

BELOW: DAVID INTRODUCED THE IDEA THAT THE GRAY HULK WAS YET ANOTHER OF BRUCE BANNER'S MULTIPLE PERSONALITIES.

Classic comics series cannot long stray from their roots, and, despite the commercial success of his Hulk stories for nearly a decade, David came under pressure to return the Hulk to his traditional persona. David wrote a savage green Hulk for a while, but soon left the series. Before he did so, however, he capped his run on the book with a tragic note: Betty Ross Banner died, apparently from radiation poisoning as a result of being exposed to the Hulk for so long.

This, though, soon proved not to be the case. David's successor, writer Joe Casey, revealed that it was the Abomination, the Hulk's old enemy, who had somehow given Betty the lethal dose of radiation.

Wise enough to know that comic book deaths are rarely irreversible, Peter David left Betty's body preserved in a sort of post-mortem suspended animation, so that later writers, if they so chose, could easily resurrect her, as he had done with her father.

In recent years comics companies have often started the numbering of a series over again with issue #1 as a gimmick to boost sales from collectors. So it was that Hulk: Volume Two had its first issue (April 1999), with John Byrne back as writer. Not only did Byrne bring back Tyrannus, but he also revived the idea of Bruce Banner wandering nomadically through the United States, trying to stay a step ahead of the law, along the lines of the 1970s TV series. Although Byrne again left the series after a short time, the writers who have followed him have continued this *Fugitive* motif.

One of them, British writer Paul Jenkins, took the multiple personality concept to its limit, revealing that Banner's psyche was so fragmented that it held a seemingly limitless number of potential alternate personalities, including one that was far more evil than any version of the Hulk readers had seen yet.

In these early years of the new century, the Incredible Hulk has been dominated by veteran comics writer Bruce Jones, working with artists John Romita Jr. and Mike Deodato Jr. Jones crafted a years-long story arc in which the Hulk was blamed for the accidental death of a child, forcing Bruce Banner to go on the run, pursued by a mysterious conspiracy seeking to exploit the Hulk. Along the way, Hulk encountered such old adversaries as the Leader, the Abomination, and the "Absorbing Man." Moreover, after enough time had passed for it to be a surprise, Jones brought Betty Ross Banner back from the dead. (Meanwhile, new versions of the Hulk and Betty are featured in Marvel's the Ultimates, an alternate reality version of the Avengers.)

The classic quartet of Stan Lee's Hulk characters—Banner, Betty, General Ross, and Talbot—all turned up in the 2003 *Hulk* live-action movie, directed by the acclaimed Ang Lee of *Crouching Tiger, Hidden Dragon* fame.

While actor Eric Bana played Bruce Banner (who got to retain his real first name), the Hulk was an entirely computer-animated creation, made possible by the amazing recent advances in CGI technology. No longer would filmmakers need to use a strongman painted green, but Lou Ferrigno did turn up in the movie in a delightful cameo with Stan Lee.

Written by James Schamus and others, Ang Lee's movie drew heavily on the multiple personality disorder interpretation that Bill Mantlo had introduced and Peter David had popularized. Nick Nolte played Bruce's abusive father, who was named David in apparent homage to the television series; this new David Banner also gained the powers of the Hulk's longtime foe in the comics, the Absorbing Man. It was commercially successful enough that Marvel has announced its intentions to co-produce a sequel.

Back in the comics Bruce Jones left the Incredible Hulk to be followed in 2005 by the returning Peter David, who had recently written one of the character's finest stories ever, "Hulk: The End," depicting a possible denouement for the Hulk's saga on an Earth after nuclear war.

But today the Incredible Hulk is far from his own end. In comics, television, film, and DVDs, the Hulk is better known today than at any time in his past. Created at the height of the Cold War of the 1960s, the Hulk has remained the most celebrated antihero in twenty-first-century popular culture.

OPPOSITE: PETER DAVID WROTE "HULK: THE END" AND THEN RETURNED TO THE SERIES IN 2005.

BELOW: HULK SAT ALONE AMID DESOLATION CAUSED BY NUCLEAR HOLOCAUST IN THE FINAL PANEL OF DAVID'S "HULK: THE END."

SEPT
60¢ U.K. 25 P
#1
A MARVEL® COMICS LIMITED SERIES
APPROVED BY THE COMICS CODE AUTHORITY
WOLVERINE™

WOLVERINE

MARVEL'S POPULAR MUTANT WITH THE MYSTERIOUS PAST

It has been claimed that no Super Hero created at any comics company or in any medium has matched the enduring popularity and iconic power of the great characters created at Marvel in the 1960s. There is one clear exception to the rule, who first appeared in the mid-1970s and has since become one of the most famous Super Heroes in comics, television, and the movies: the mutant with the invincible, slashing claws, "Wolverine."

The history of Wolverine is inseparable from the history of the series for which he was created, the X-Men. Though Wolverine has now starred in many comics series of his own, it is as a member of the X-Men that most people first encountered him.

Debuting in their own comic book in 1963, the X-Men were created by Stan Lee and Jack Kirby, who had also originated the Fantastic Four, the Incredible Hulk, and the Mighty Thor in the two previous years. The two partners collaborated on plotting the stories, Kirby drew them in his trademark dynamic style, and Lee scripted their vivid dialogue.

What made the X-Men different from the other Marvel heroes, first and foremost, was that they were mutants. Mutation, an alteration in a living being's genetic structure, takes place in real life and is one of the means by which evolution occurs. Science fiction writers had employed the concept of mutants long before Stan Lee built a comic book series upon the concept. In Lee and Kirby's X-Men, mutation could endow people with superhuman powers.

Whereas the Fantastic Four, Spider-Man, and the Hulk gained their superpowers through inadvertent exposure to radiation, the X-Men were mutants born with the genetic potential for superpowers, which usually emerged in adolescence. In the Marvel Universe, mutants were not ordinary human beings who acquired superpowers by chance; they were members of a newly evolving superhuman race, not *Homo sapien*s, but *Homo superior*s.

The founder of the X-Men was Professor Charles Xavier, a man who was confined to a wheelchair and yet had the most powerful mind on Earth: not only was he a genius, but he had greater telepathic powers than anyone on the planet, enabling him to read minds and communicate with others mentally.

OPPOSITE: WHEN THE FOUR-ISSUE WOLVERINE MINI-SERIES APPEARED IN SEPTEMBER 1982, THE CHARACTER WAS ALREADY A FAVORITE OF X-MEN FANS.

THE STRANGEST SUPER-HEROES OF ALL!
APPROVED BY THE COMICS CODE AUTHORITY
1 SEPT.
IND.
MARVEL COMICS GROUP 12¢
the X-MEN
IN THE SENSATIONAL FANTASTIC FOUR STYLE!
DON'T MISS THIS FABULOUS FIRST ISSUE!
X-MEN VERSUS MAGNETO EARTH'S MOST POWERFUL SUPER VILLAIN!!

OPPOSITE: THE *X-MEN* #1 INTRODUCED THE SECOND SUPER HERO TEAM CO-CREATED BY STAN LEE AND JACK KIRBY.

LEFT: ALTHOUGH OUTCASTS FROM SOCIETY, THE MUTANT X-MEN HAVE PROTECTED HUMANITY FROM MAGNETO, WHO BELIEVES MUTANTS SHOULD CONTROL THE EARTH.

Decades before J. K. Rowling introduced her school for teenage magicians in her Harry Potter series, Stan Lee and Jack Kirby had co-created their own school for teens with extraordinary powers. Charles Xavier found teenage superhuman mutants and gathered them into the private school he had established at his mansion in New York State's Westchester County. At "Professor Xavier's School for Gifted Youngsters," Xavier secretly trained his students to master their superpowers. Xavier also molded some of his charges into a team of costumed champions who used their powers to help "normal" human beings.

Xavier was well aware that humans had the tendency to fear, hate, and even persecute those who were different from themselves, including the new mutant race that was evolving in their midst. Moreover, some mutants would justify those fears. The most notorious example was Xavier's former friend "Magneto," who believed that superpowered mutants were naturally superior to the rest of humanity and deserved to rule them. But even though the rest of humanity feared and distrusted them, the X-Men battled to defend them from Magneto and other mutant menaces.

Charles Xavier was a visionary, who had a dream of a world in which mutants and normal humans would coexist in peace. Founding the X-Men was the first step towards achieving that dream.

The brilliance of Lee and Kirby's concept was that anyone and any group who regarded themselves as outsiders in society could identify with the X-Men. Moreover, though the X-Men were outcasts, by banding together they created their own community or "family." This too was an appealing concept for readers: no matter how alone you felt, you could find and bond with others like yourself.

Xavier's original team of X-Men included "Cyclops," "Marvel Girl" (Jean Grey, now known as "Phoenix"), the winged "Angel," the "Beast," and "Iceman." Lee and Kirby collaborated on the series' first seventeen

ABOVE: MARVEL GIRL, THE BEAST, CYCLOPS, ANGEL, AND ICEMAN WERE GIVEN A NEW LOOK IN ISSUE #39.

OPPOSITE: A BATTLE BETWEEN HULK AND NEWCOMER WOLVERINE SPANNED ISSUES #180–181 IN LATE 1974.

issues and were succeeded by other writers and artists. One of the series' high points came at the end of the 1960s with a run of stories by writer Roy Thomas and the great comics illustrator Neal Adams.

Yet hard as it may seem to believe today, X-Men was not originally a commercial success and the book was canceled after the March 1970 issue. Throughout the 1960s, X-Men had only been a second- or even third-tier title, overshadowed by the brilliance of Fantastic Four and other, more prominent Marvel series.

Nonetheless, X-Men was a favorite among many Marvel readers and the new generation of comics writers, starting with Roy Thomas, who had been inspired by Stan Lee's revolutionary work in the 1960s. Members of the X-Men continued to guest star in other Marvel books, the Beast won his own short-lived series, and Marvel kept reprinting old X-Men stories.

In the early 1970s, Stan Lee became Marvel's publisher, and former X-Men writer Roy Thomas succeeded him as editor in chief. Intent on reviving the X-Men, Thomas came up with an idea for revamping the concept for a new decade: The X-Men would become an international team, with members drawn from around the world. It was Thomas's new concept for the X-Men that led to the creation of Wolverine.

Wolverine is a character who has many "fathers." Thomas says that he had the idea that one of the X-Men should be Canadian and presented it to writer Len Wein. Thomas and Wein have each claimed to have come up with the name Wolverine. It was a good name: real wolverines are small, stocky, but fierce animals, surprisingly dangerous for their size, have sharp claws used for digging, and are native to Canada and the northern United States.

Intending that he would be used later in the revived X-Men, Wein introduced Wolverine in *Incredible Hulk* #180 (October 1974) and the following issue. Marvel's art director John Romita Sr. created the character's visual appearance and costume, but it was regular Hulk artist Herb Trimpe who drew the two-part story, which was inked by the late Jack Abel.

In this story the Hulk, regarded worldwide as a menace, had strayed into Canada. The Canadian government sends their super-powered operative, "Weapon X," to stop the monster. Weapon X was also code-named Wolverine. At five feet, three inches tall, Wolverine was dwarfed by the immense Hulk. But the ferocious Wolverine was far from intimidated. Three retractable claws, each a foot long, would emerge from the back of each of his hands. (On "popping" out, the claws created a sound like a switchblade: "SNIKT!") Each claw was

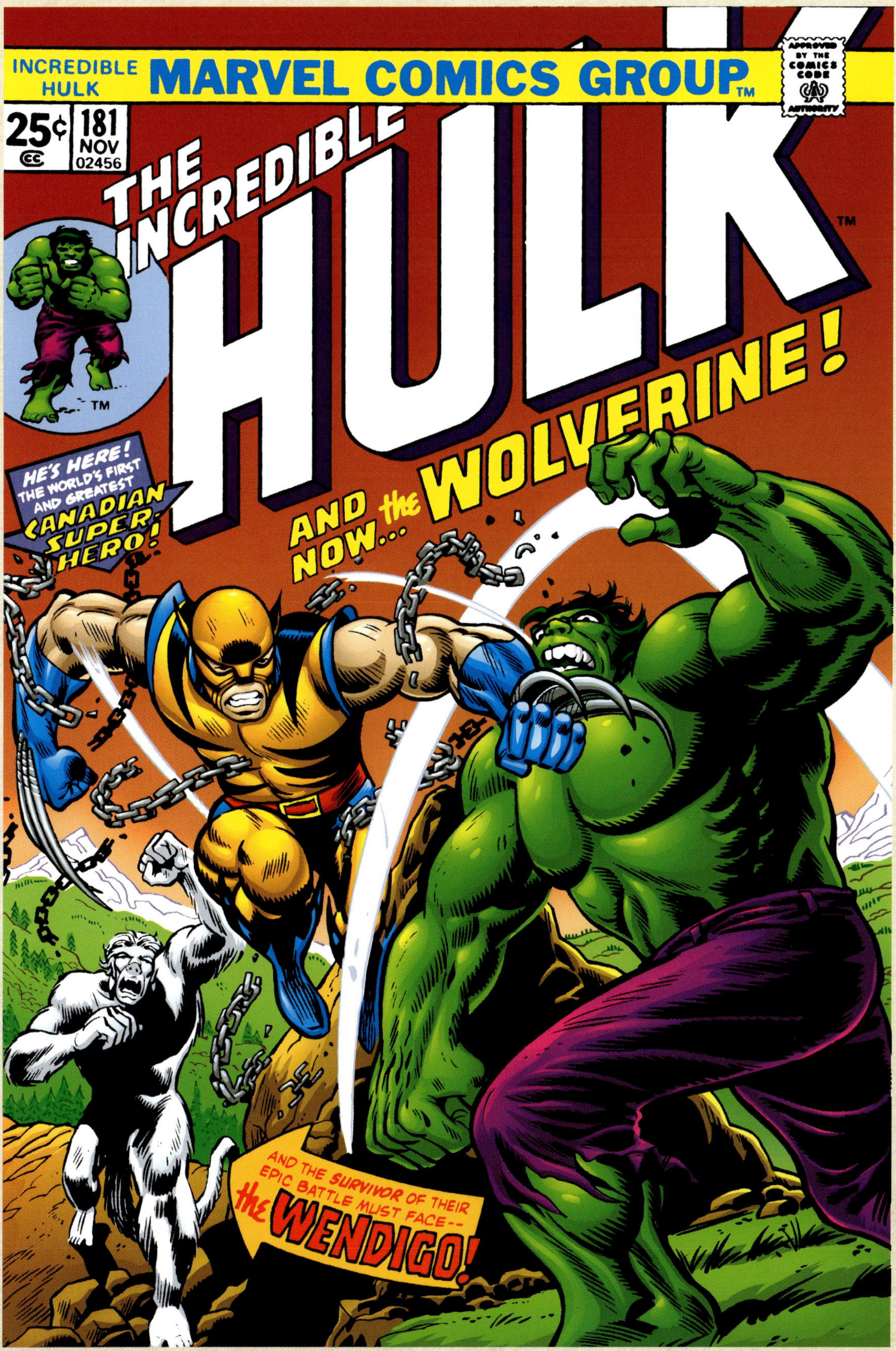

INCREDIBLE HULK
MARVEL COMICS GROUP
APPROVED BY THE COMICS CODE AUTHORITY
25¢
181 NOV 02456
THE INCREDIBLE HULK
HE'S HERE! THE WORLD'S FIRST AND GREATEST CANADIAN SUPER-HERO!
AND NOW... the WOLVERINE!
AND THE SURVIVOR OF THEIR EPIC BATTLE MUST FACE-- the WENDIGO!

RIGHT: WHEN THE X-MEN STORMED BACK INTO THE MARVEL UNIVERSE IN *GIANT-SIZE X-MEN* #1 (1975), WOLVERINE CAME WITH THEM.

OPPOSITE: READERS GOT THEIR FIRST LOOK AT WOLVERINE'S TEMPER WHEN CHARLES XAVIER RECRUITED HIM FOR THE X-MEN.

infused with adamantium, a fictional steel alloy that Roy Thomas had introduced in another Marvel series, the Avengers, that was absolutely indestructible. (Originally Wein intended that the claws were made entirely of adamantium; as we shall see, this later proved untrue.) The Hulk was far stronger than his opponent, but Wolverine's sharp adamantium claws could penetrate even the Hulk's thick hide.

As it turned out, Wolverine was unable to capture or defeat the Hulk, because they were both confronted by a third opponent, a legendary man-eating monster called a "Wendigo."

In the following year, 1975, Marvel relaunched the X-Men in the double-sized *Giant-Size X-Men* #1, written by Wein and drawn by the popular artist Dave Cockrum. According to their story, the original X-Men were held captive on the mysterious island of "Krakoa," which proved to be an enormous living creature, the world's biggest mutant. Only team leader Cyclops managed to escape and return to Professor Xavier at his mansion. Xavier set about recruiting a new team of X-Men from around the world, including such now familiar characters as "Storm" and "Nightcrawler." Xavier also traveled to Canada and invited Wolverine to join.

Wolverine's superior angrily protested that after all the money the Canadian government had invested in Wolverine, he could not abruptly quit. Having had his fill of working for government bureaucrats, Wolverine angrily lashed out with his claws, severing his superior's necktie. Wolverine accepted Xavier's invitation and traveled back to Westchester County with him.

Xavier's new X-Men team headed to Krakoa, where they freed their predecessors.

The regular-sized X-Men comic series began again with issue #94 (August 1975), picking up the numbering from where the original X-Men comic had left off. In this first new issue, the original X-Men, except for Cyclops, announced that they were leaving to follow new pursuits. Cyclops was made Xavier's "deputy leader" of the new X-Men, which included Wolverine.

Though Wein plotted this first issue, it was his last. Busy writing other Marvel series, Wein ceded X-Men to a Marvel newcomer, Chris Claremont, who dialogued issue #94 and took over both plot and script with issue #95.

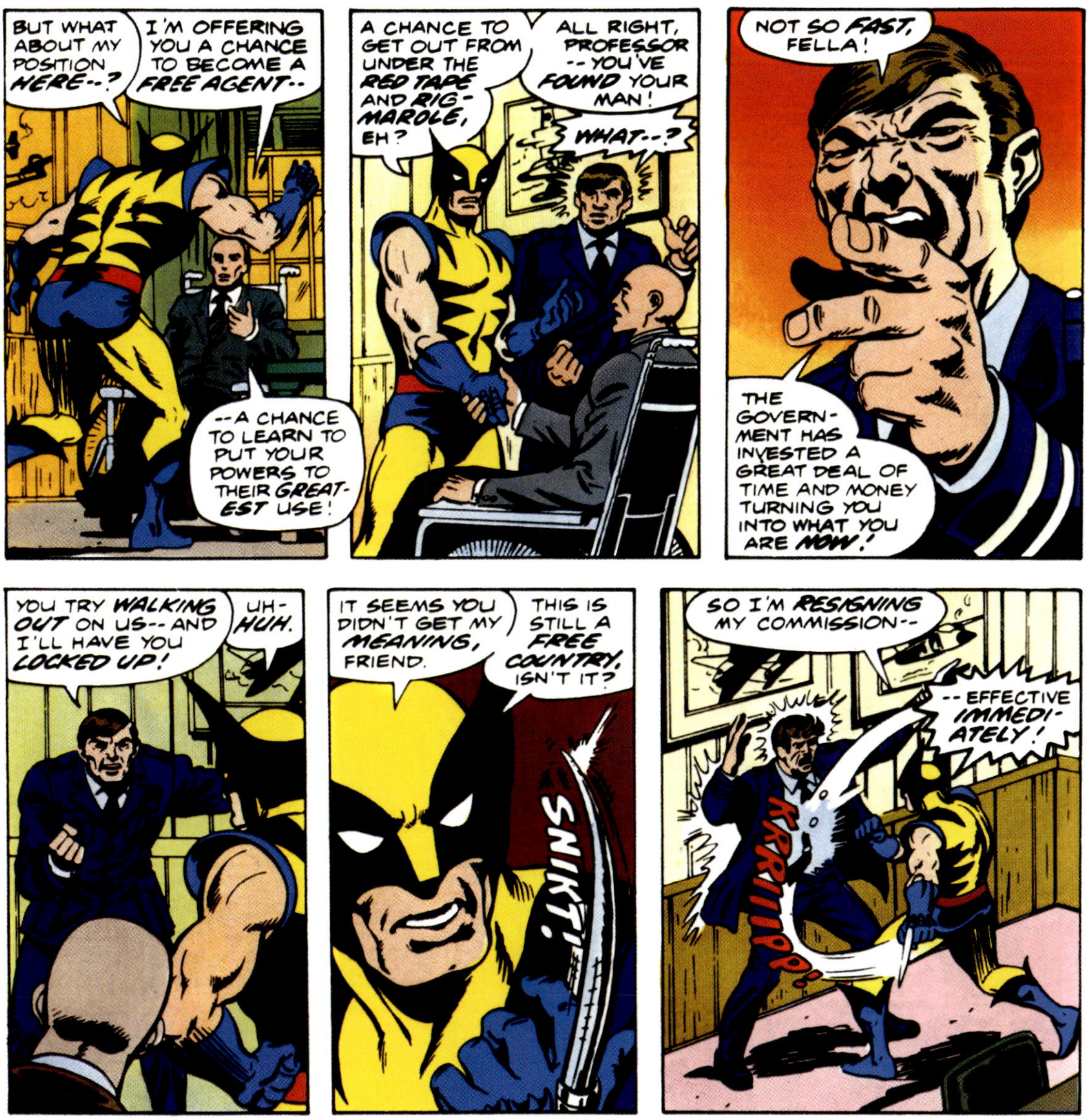

This was a major turning point in X-Men history. Claremont not only made his reputation as one of American comics' leading writers on X-Men, but he is the writer most responsible for turning X-Men into the commercial blockbuster it is today. Claremont has written more X-Men stories than anyone else in the series' history: he scripted every issue from 1975 to 1990 and is still writing the Uncanny X-Men in 2005.

Chris Claremont is also the person most responsible for molding Wolverine into the character we know today. First he took the character in directions that his co-creator, Len Wein, had not planned. Wein intended Wolverine to be a teenager, as the original X-Men had been. Claremont played Wolverine as an older character, an adult with a long, mysterious past. Wein also considered Wolverine's adamantium claws part of his costume, not actually part of him. As Claremont has pointed out in interviews, if that were so, then what would make Wolverine so special? The Canadian government could have simply outfitted another operative with gloves that sprout claws. Perhaps more importantly, if the claws were not part of Wolverine, then what made him a mutant?

Dave Cockrum stayed on as X-Men artist and first showed readers what Wolverine looked like unmasked. In the world of Super Hero comics, heroic faces tend to look alike, but Cockrum devised one of the most distinctive faces in the genre for Wolverine. Oddly, Wolverine's hairstyle mimicked his costume, forming into two devil-like horns, perhaps symbolizing the dark side of his personality. When he was out of costume, Cockrum and Claremont decided to dress him in western-style clothing. There was something of the cowboy in Wolverine, albeit one from western Canada.

Claremont and Cockrum also showed Wolverine popping his claws from his bare hands. It was now shockingly clear that the claws were part of him.

But how could even a mutant naturally have claws made of adamantium steel? And why didn't he bleed when the sharp claws emerged from beneath his skin?

Claremont eventually developed the answers. Unknown parties had somehow infused Wolverine's skeleton with adamantium, binding it to the organic molecules of his bones. Hence, his entire skeleton was as unbreakable as his claws. What made Wolverine a mutant was not his adamantium-laced skeleton, but the superhuman trait that made the adamantium bonding process possible.

Wolverine's principal mutant power was his "healing factor": injuries he sustained would heal within minutes, even seconds. That was how Wolverine could survive the process that bonded the adamantium to his bones. It was why he could "pop" his claws without any lasting damage to himself. Since wounds did him no lasting harm, Wolverine's healing ability made him even harder to stop in battle.

Furthermore, as Claremont explained over the years, Wolverine's healing factor greatly retarded his aging. It was impossible to tell just how old Wolverine was, and Claremont would eventually hint that Wolverine was alive back in the nineteenth century.

Claremont also established that Wolverine had superhumanly acute senses, especially that of smell. He could track a quarry by scent alone. In this and other ways, Wolverine was created as a man with animal-like traits, as his name suggests.

While Cockrum drew X-Men in these early years, he tended to play the short, feisty Wolverine for comedy (rather like the dwarf Gimli in *The Lord of the Rings* movies). Cockrum preferred Nightcrawler, and Claremont did not yet realize Wolverine's full potential.

Still, it was during this period that Claremont established that Wolverine was not simply comically hot-tempered, but dangerously so. Wolverine could abruptly go into a "berserker rage," in which his violent nature overwhelmed his rationality. At one point early on, Wolverine confessed to the other X-Men that for years the Canadian government had subjected him to treatments to cure him of these rages, all in vain; what is more, Wolverine said ominously that he was glad they hadn't succeeded. Wolverine enjoyed giving in to his animalistic nature.

This speech by Wolverine pointed the way to his character's future. The real impetus for further developing Wolverine as a character was

OPPOSITE: DAVE COCKRUM WAS THE ARTIST RESPONSIBLE FOR WOLVERINE'S UNMASKED APPEARANCE.

OPPOSITE: WOLVERINE ENJOYED GIVING IN TO HIS ANIMALISTIC BERSERKER RAGE.

the arrival of John Byrne as X-Men artist and co-plotter. Born in England (as was Claremont), Byrne grew up in Canada and hence took special interest in his countryman Wolverine.

In issue #108 (February 1978), the Canadian government sent "Weapon Alpha" to try to bring Wolverine back by force. Weapon Alpha was James MacDonald Hudson, later known as "Guardian," a character Byrne had created before becoming a comics professional. As Claremont, Byrne, and others elaborated upon Wolverine's back story, it was revealed that Hudson, a Canadian scientist, and his wife Heather had found Wolverine in the Canadian wilderness years before. At that time Wolverine was a feral creature, behaving more like an animal than a human being, apparently having forgotten how to speak; he already had the adamantium claws. The Hudsons nursed him back to mental health, but Wolverine had no memory of his past and no idea how he got his adamantium claws. James Hudson recruited Wolverine into the team of superhuman operatives called "Alpha Flight," which he was organizing for the Canadian government. Hudson, this time assisted by the rest of Alpha Flight, tried again to capture Wolverine in *Uncanny X-Men* #120–121 (April to May 1979). But eventually Hudson and Wolverine made peace, and Wolverine still regards the Hudsons as two of his closest friends. Indeed, it has become clear that Wolverine was once in love with Heather, but would not come between the couple. (Byrne later created an Alpha Flight series for Marvel, and issue #34 showed how the Hudsons found Wolverine.)

Another landmark moment in Wolverine's history occurred in *Uncanny X-Men* #116 (December 1978) when Claremont and Byrne sent the X-Men down to the "Savage Land," Marvel's own prehistoric lost world. Trying to invade the fortress of their enemies, Storm, Nightcrawler, and Wolverine found their way blocked by a guard. Readers did not see what Wolverine did to the guard, but Nightcrawler's and Storm's reactions made it clear, Wolverine had killed him.

Up until this time it was tradition that Super Heroes never took a human life. But Claremont and Byrne agreed that Wolverine should break the tradition. Claremont regarded Wolverine as a former soldier, and soldiers killed when they found it necessary. Marvel editor in chief Jim Shooter objected strenuously to Byrne and Claremont's implications that Wolverine killed opponents, but Shooter's efforts were ultimately in vain. For years Marvel had been publishing Conan the Barbarian, a sword and sorcery hero who killed in combat. Now Super Hero comics were moving into a more mature phase, and this episode in the Savage Land was one of the signs of change.

Claremont and Byrne took the X-Men to Japan in issue #118 (February 1979), where they introduced Wolverine to his first love interest, a demure, very traditional Japanese woman named Mariko Yashida. As Claremont and Byrne have explained in interviews, they were following the idea that "opposites attract." The quiet Mariko seemed the total opposite of Wolverine.

OPPOSITE: A PORTION OF WOLVERINE'S MURKY PAST BECAME CLEAR WHEN X-MEN READERS WERE INTRODUCED TO JAMES MACDONALD, A.K.A. WEAPON ALPHA.

BELOW: MARVEL COMICS MATURED WHEN WOLVERINE KILLED A SENTRY IN *UNCANNY X-MEN* #116, ALTHOUGH THE DEATH WAS NOT SHOWN TO READERS.

RIGHT: WOLVERINE SURPRISED READERS WITH HIS SENSITIVE SIDE IN ISSUE #109.

OPPOSITE: (TOP) WOLVERINE'S INTEREST IN JAPANESE CULTURE WAS INTENSIFIED BY HIS APPRECIATION OF MARIKO'S BEAUTY; (BOTTOM) JOHN BYRNE'S MEMORABLE WOLVERINE PANEL FROM ISSUE #132.

Yet Claremont and Byrne were also using Mariko to show a different side of Wolverine. Even back in issue #109 they had Wolverine surprise Storm—and the readers—when he set out to hunt a deer, not to kill it with a swipe of his claws, but merely to touch it. There was a side of Wolverine that longed for beauty, for peace of mind, for love, all of which Mariko represented to him.

Through this storyline, Claremont also first established Wolverine's interest in Japanese culture. Long before the current American boom in manga (Japanese comics) sales, Claremont was one of the American comics creators fascinated by Japanese popular culture, and this would prove to be a major influence on Wolverine's evolution.

It was also in this story that Wolverine revealed his real name, or as "real" a name as someone who could not remember so much of his past could have: Logan. That was all, and it was not clear whether it was his first or last name. Claremont and Byrne had named the character after Mount Logan in western Canada.

Perhaps the Wolverine sequence that readers best remember from Claremont and Byrne's classic collaboration on X-Men came during the celebrated "Dark Phoenix Saga." Various X-Men had been taken prisoner by the "Hellfire Club" in their Manhattan mansion, but not Wolverine, who had fallen into the sewers and been presumed dead. Issue #132 (April 1980) ended with Byrne's most memorable shot of Wolverine, his face twisted in rage as he rises, covered with grime, from the sewer waters, vowing vengeance. In the following issue, Wolverine single-handedly invaded the Hellfire Club mansion, lashing out viciously at the uniformed mercenaries who tried in vain to stop him. If Byrne and Claremont had treated the death of the Savage Land guard in an understated manner, here they allowed Wolverine to explode into violent fury in clear view.

At one point in this issue, Wolverine defeated a lone guard by merely giving him a speech about the lethal nature of his adamantium claws; the guard was terrified into submission. The sequence was Byrne and Claremont's homage to a famous moment in the movie *Dirty Harry*, and it demonstratred how Wolverine was coming to resemble Clint Eastwood's onscreen persona.

Even before they teamed up on X-Men, Byrne and Claremont had co-created another important part of the Wolverine legend. They had first collaborated on Iron Fist, a comic about a martial arts Super Hero, and

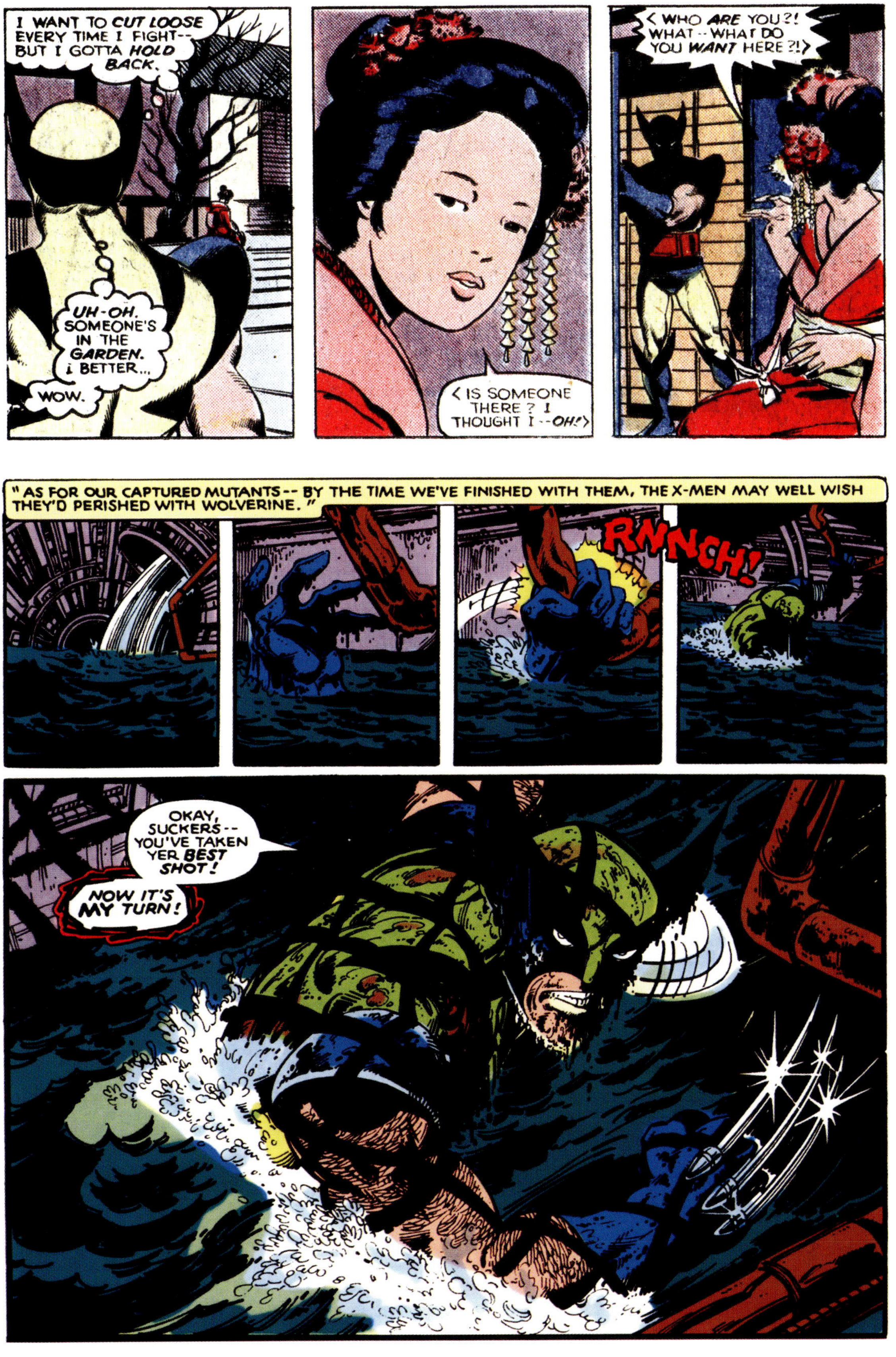
I WANT TO CUT LOOSE EVERY TIME I FIGHT-- BUT I GOTTA HOLD BACK.
UH-OH. SOMEONE'S IN THE GARDEN. I BETTER...
WOW.
<IS SOMEONE THERE? I THOUGHT I --OH!>
<WHO ARE YOU?! WHAT--WHAT DO YOU WANT HERE?!>
"AS FOR OUR CAPTURED MUTANTS-- BY THE TIME WE'VE FINISHED WITH THEM, THE X-MEN MAY WELL WISH THEY'D PERISHED WITH WOLVERINE."
RNNCH!
OKAY, SUCKERS-- YOU'VE TAKEN YER BEST SHOT!
NOW IT'S MY TURN!

in that series' issue #14 (August 1977) they introduced a villain named "Sabretooth." HIs physical appearance and ferocity made Sabretooth seem much like Wolverine, although he lacked his adamantium skeleton and claws. Claremont would later establish that Sabretooth was Wolverine's archenemy, and they battled repeatedly over the years. Sabretooth was Wolverine without any redeeming qualities, a man who had given himself over to his bestial nature. Sabretooth contemptuously referred to Wolverine as "boy," as if Sabretooth were his elder. In fact, as Byrne has often admitted, Sabretooth was intended to be Wolverine's father, though neither he nor Claremont ever made this explicit. Nonetheless, enough readers picked up on this subtext that later writers decided to change it, making Sabretooth Wolverine's former partner in his days as a secret agent.

Though Byrne and Claremont had revealed a more civilized side of the character, Wolverine still hovered on the brink of madness. In Byrne's final issue (#143, March 1981), when Nightcrawler innocently spoke to Mariko, Wolverine suddenly became furious, lashing out at his teammate with his claws.

Claremont realized that he could not leave Wolverine like this; the character had to evolve further. It was in the first Wolverine limited series (four issues, dated September to December 1982) that Claremont defined the personality of Wolverine as readers have known him ever since.

BELOW: WOLVERINE'S RELATIONSHIP WITH MARIKO MADE HIM APPEAR CIVILIZED, BUT JEALOUSY FURTHER COMPLICATED HIS STRUGGLE TO CONTROL HIS RAGE.

OPPOSITE: FRANK MILLER'S COVERS FOR ISSUES #2-4 OF THE WOLVERINE MINI-SERIES.

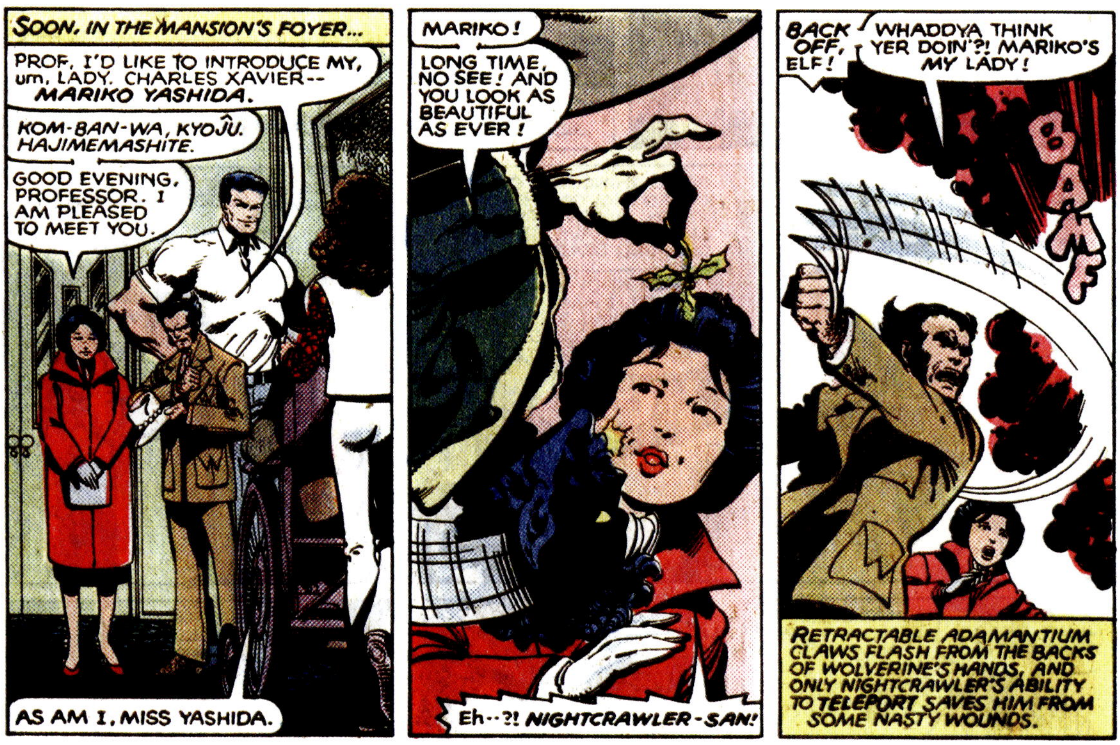

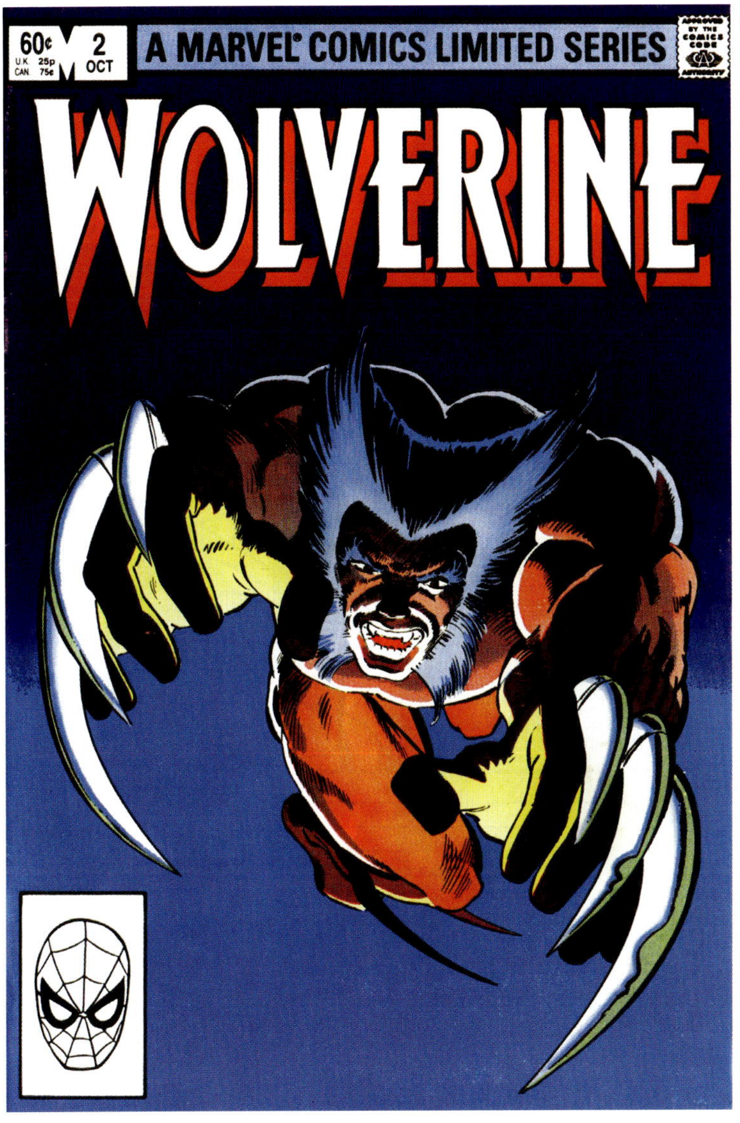

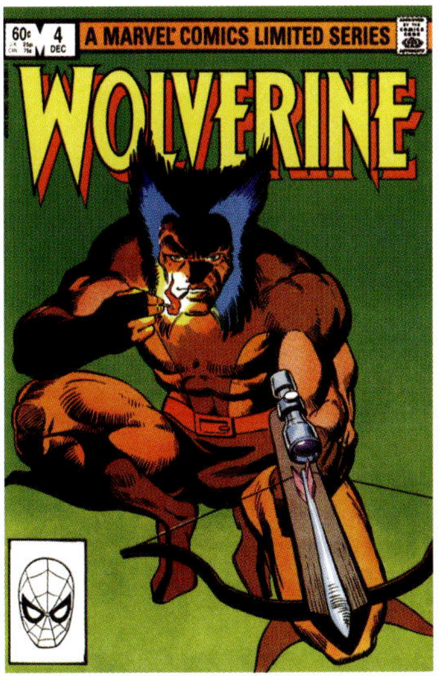

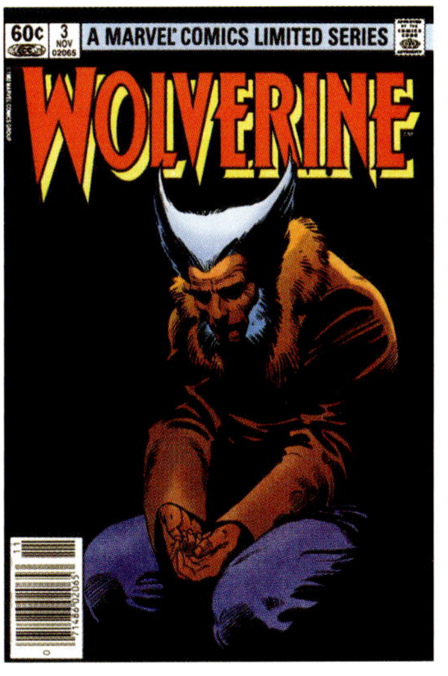

Collaborating with Claremont was another of the most important comics creators of their generation, Frank Miller, who co-plotted and illustrated this mini-series. Miller had first made his mark in the early 1980s on Marvel's Daredevil, for which he created the female ninja "Elektra." Following Wolverine, Miller would go on to revamp Batman for a new generation in The Dark Knight Returns and create the crime comic Sin City, which in 2005 became a movie co-directed by Miller himself.

As Elektra showed, Miller too had a strong interest in Japanese culture. Claremont and Miller's Wolverine mini-series took the character back to Japan, where he encountered his beloved Mariko's father, Lord Shingen, head of the Yakuza, Japan's network of organized crime. Shingen humiliated Wolverine in combat, leaving the mutant feeling more like a beaten animal than a man. Wolverine recognized that he must control his inner demons if he was to defeat Shingen: the man must master the beast within. Through the traditional disciplines of the samurai warrior, Wolverine succeeded, and his rematch with Shingen ended in the crime lord's death. The four-issue series ended with the X-Men receiving their invitations to Logan's marriage to Mariko. (The marriage never took place due to the interference of one of the X-Men's longtime adversaries, "Mastermind.")

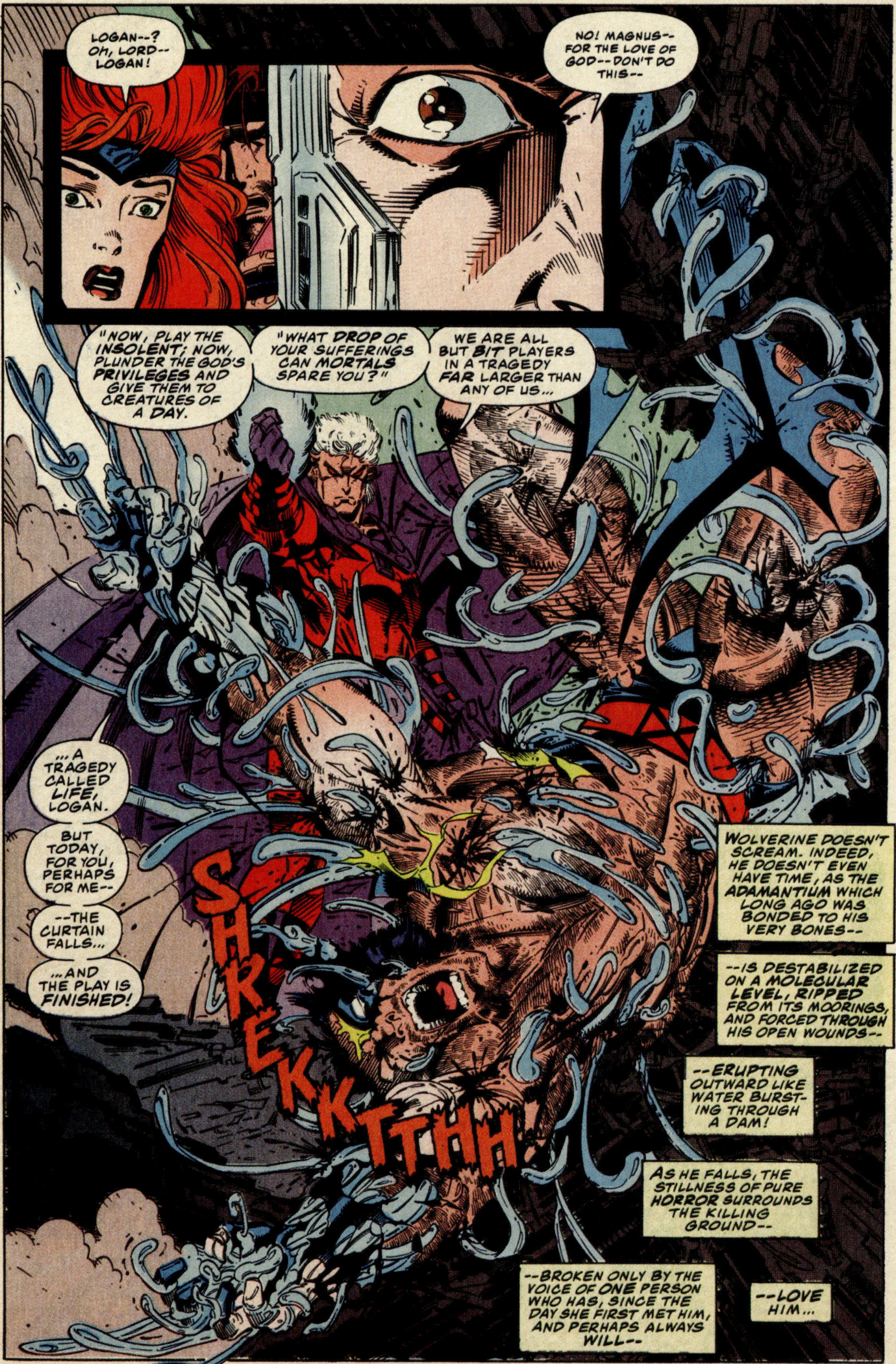

LOGAN--? OH, LORD-- LOGAN!
NO! MAGNUS-- FOR THE LOVE OF GOD--DON'T DO THIS--
"NOW, PLAY THE INSOLENT; NOW, PLUNDER THE GOD'S PRIVILEGES AND GIVE THEM TO CREATURES OF A DAY.
"WHAT DROP OF YOUR SUFFERINGS CAN MORTALS SPARE YOU?"
WE ARE ALL BUT BIT PLAYERS IN A TRAGEDY FAR LARGER THAN ANY OF US...
...A TRAGEDY CALLED LIFE, LOGAN.
BUT TODAY, FOR YOU, PERHAPS FOR ME--
--THE CURTAIN FALLS...
...AND THE PLAY IS FINISHED!
SHREKKKTTHH!
WOLVERINE DOESN'T SCREAM. INDEED, HE DOESN'T EVEN HAVE TIME, AS THE ADAMANTIUM WHICH LONG AGO WAS BONDED TO HIS VERY BONES--
--IS DESTABILIZED ON A MOLECULAR LEVEL, RIPPED FROM ITS MOORINGS, AND FORCED THROUGH HIS OPEN WOUNDS--
--ERUPTING OUTWARD LIKE WATER BURST-ING THROUGH A DAM!
AS HE FALLS, THE STILLNESS OF PURE HORROR SURROUNDS THE KILLING GROUND--
--BROKEN ONLY BY THE VOICE OF ONE PERSON WHO HAS, SINCE THE DAY SHE FIRST MET HIM, AND PERHAPS ALWAYS WILL--
--LOVE HIM...

THE ROADS NOT TAKEN

Mutants in the Marvel Universe do not choose to become what they are; mutation is their genetic destiny, determined by fate before they were born. However, these mutants do decide what to do with their superhuman abilities. Wolverine chose a very different path than his greatest adversaries took.

As chronicled in the first Wolverine limited series (September to December 1982), through sheer force of will, Logan finally achieved a measure of control over the beast within himself. That control is not perfect and probably never will be, but it allows Logan to function normally within the rest of human—and mutant—society.

Had Logan not followed this path in life, he would have ended up like his perennial rival, Victor Creed, alias Sabretooth. Not only does Sabretooth look like a bigger, blond-haired version of Wolverine, but he also has the same mutant powers. Like Wolverine, Sabretooth joined a team of fellow mutants: the assassins called the "Marauders."

If Wolverine's potential for madness is genetic in origin, then Sabretooth seems to share the same genetic flaw. But whereas Logan has consistently sought to transcend his animal nature, Creed has succumbed to his inner beast. Sabretooth has sunk so low as to become a serial killer, murdering humans for sport. Each year he hunts Wolverine down on the latter's birthday, trying once again to kill him. Perhaps Sabretooth is so obsessed with Wolverine because he recognizes in Logan the kind of person he refuses to become.

Sabretooth is out to wreak havoc and foment chaos. Another of Wolverine's prime adversaries has a different goal: to impose order on mutant-kind and the rest of humanity, whether they agree with him or not. This is Magneto, who has been Xavier's and the X-Men's leading foe since the original *X-Men* #1 (September 1963).

Imprisoned in the Nazi death camp at Auschwitz as a child, Magneto knew first hand of the horrors of man's inhumanity to man. Following World War II, Magneto discovered that he could mentally control the force of magnetism. He realized that he was a member of the emerging race of "Homo superior," superhuman mutants. As a young man he befriended Charles Xavier, and they debated the future of the mutants in human society. Magneto was determined that the mutant race would not suffer the fate of the Nazis' victims. Whereas Xavier advocated peaceful coexistence, Magneto came to believe that mutants could only ensure their own safety by taking control of the world by force. He has repeatedly attempted to conquer the planet, only to be thwarted by the X-Men, including Wolverine.

Since adamantium is a form of steel, Wolverine is particularly vulnerable to Magneto's powers. Hence, Magneto once succeeded in magnetically drawing the adamantium molecules out of Wolverine's skeleton (In *X-Men* [second series] #25, October 1993).

Over the decades different writers have interpreted Magneto in sharply different ways. The character's co-creators, Stan Lee and Jack Kirby, depicted Magneto as a ruthless terrorist, willing to destroy an entire nation with a nuclear device. Longtime X-Men writer Chris Claremont has sought to turn Magneto from terrorist to "statesman," as he has put it, showing Magneto undergoing a crisis of conscience and again allying himself with Xavier. At one point, when Xavier was physically incapacitated, the Professor even appointed Magneto to take charge of his school for mutants. More recent writers, such as Grant Morrison and Mark Millar, have depicted Magneto as more sinister than ever, a racist demagogue willing to enslave or exterminate the human race.

MAGNETO'S ABILITY TO MANIPULATE METAL MAKES HIM A PARTICULARLY DANGEROUS ENEMY TO ADAMANTIUM-LACED WOLVERINE, WHO NEARLY DIED FOLLOWING THIS CONFRONTATION IN X-MEN [SECOND SERIES] #25.

‹ THAT, GAIJIN... ›
‹... REMAINS TO BE SEEN. ›
WE MOVE AS ONE...
... BLADES HISSING THROUGH THE AIR...
... AS WE PASS.
I CUT DEEP.
SHINGEN CUTS DEEPER.
I'M HURT BAD. HE KNOWS IT.
BUT NO QUARTER IS ASKED...

It took a while for other writers who guest starred Wolverine in their stories to recognize that the character had changed, but eventually everyone adopted Claremont's definitive characterization. Wolverine was no longer a walking time bomb capable of exploding at any moment at either friend or foe. Now Claremont portrayed him as a veteran warrior, who had, over the years, been a soldier, a spy, and a Super Hero. Unlike some of the younger X-Men, Wolverine was an experienced fighter, not only formidable in hand-to-hand combat but a cunning strategist as well. As his motto went, Wolverine was "the best there is at what [he does]."

Now Wolverine no longer needed the other X-Men around to make sure he did not go berserk. He could and did go on solo adventures. In fact, Wolverine started to show an unexpected paternal side, initially by taking the X-Men's youngest member, teenager Kitty Pryde, under his wing. Later he would even informally adopt an orphaned Japanese girl named Akiko, whom Mariko raised.

Yet though Wolverine had overcome the bestial side of his nature, he had not rid himself of it by any means. In his next mini-series, Kitty Pryde and Wolverine, these two X-Men returned to Japan, where they combated Wolverine's former mentor in the martial arts, Ogun, a reputedly immortal *ronin*, or master-less samurai. To defeat Ogun, Wolverine was forced to resort to the opposite of the strategy he used against Shingen. This time Wolverine had to voluntarily unleash the animal side of his psyche, and his berserker rage overpowered his foe. Afterwards, Wolverine felt shamed that he had let his madness overwhelm him again. He locked the "beast" within himself once more, but knew it was still there, waiting to be set free.

In interviews Claremont has explained that Wolverine sees himself as a failed samurai. Logan admires and tries to follow the traditional disciplines of the samurai, but he will never achieve perfection because of the flaw in his psyche. Claremont also speculates that this weakness, Logan's berserker tendency, may even be genetic in nature: It may be an inseparable part of what makes Wolverine a mutant. What is important, Claremont has stated, is that Wolverine heroically continues to strive for perfection, not the fact that it is beyond his grasp.

The great popularity of Wolverine's two limited series led to his starring in the lead feature of a new biweekly comic book, Marvel Comics Presents. For this new series, Claremont devised a new direction for the character. When Wolverine was not on adventures with the X-Men, he made his home base on the island of Madripoor near Indonesia. Inspired by such vintage sources as Milton Caniff's classic comic strip "Terry and the Pirates," Claremont co-created Madripoor to be a haven for criminals, divided between the modern buildings of wealthy Hightown

OPPOSITE: LORD SHINGEN HAD HIS WAY WITH WOLVERINE DURING THEIR FIRST FIGHT.

ABOVE: WOLVERINE'S RAGE HELPED HIM DEFEAT OGUN, HIS FORMER MENTOR, AND SEVERAL OTHER *RONIN*.

RIGHT: IN BARRY WINDSOR-SMITH'S "WEAPON X" STORY LINE, WOLVERINE WAS DRIVEN INSANE BY THE EXPERIMENTAL PROCESS THAT BONDED ADAMANTIUM TO HIS SKELETON.

OPPOSITE: LOGAN ESCAPED INTO THE WILDERNESS AT THE END OF WINDSOR-SMITH'S SAGA.

and the dangerous slums of Lotown. It was in the latter section that Wolverine co-owned a bar, under an alias: as "Patch" he wore an eye patch and a white dinner jacket that evoked Humphrey Bogart in *Casablanca*. Corresponding to Caniff's "Dragon Lady" was "Tyger Tiger," a sultry female crime lord who was Wolverine's sometime lover and ally against less honorable criminals.

John Buscema, a leading Marvel artist since the 1960s, drew the initial Wolverine story arc in Marvel Comics Presents. By now, Wolverine's popularity dwarfed that of any other member of the X-Men, and, inevitably, Marvel awarded him his own monthly comic book, starting with the November 1988 issue. Claremont and Buscema teamed up for this book, continuing the exploits of Wolverine in Madripoor.

But Claremont only wrote the first ten issues before giving way to other writers. Among the most noteworthy creative teams on Wolverine have been the late Archie Goodwin, one of the art form's most highly respected writers and editors, and Logan's old friend, artist John Byrne. Larry Hama had the longest run of any writer on the series, most notably working with former X-Men artist Marc Silvestri. The Wolverine comic book continues to this day, having now lasted over a decade and a half.

Claremont has always believed that much of Wolverine's power as a character lies in his mystery: readers are drawn into his world through speculating about his origins. But Claremont did not control the character, and it was inevitable that others at Marvel would succumb to the temptation to fill in the gaps in Wolverine's past.

The first creator to do so was English writer/artist Barry Windsor-Smith in his "Weapon X" story line, which was originally published in serial form in *Marvel Comics Presents* #73–84 in the early 1990s. It showed how Logan had been captured by the secret government project code-named Weapon X. At the Weapon X base somewhere in Canada, the enigmatic "Professor" subjected Wolverine to the experimental process that bonded adamantium to his skeleton. The process was so horrifically painful that it drove Logan insane: he broke free and wreaked havoc at the base before finally escaping naked into the snowy wilderness to live

YEH...
HINES...
WHAT'S UP?
UHMM...
I WAS WONDERING...
CAN I TALK TO YOU?
SURE!
IT'S JUST THAT...
I KEEP THINKING ABOUT MISTER LOGAN.
YEP. DON'T WE ALL.
AND WHAT WE'RE DOING.
YEAH.
AND THAT...
WELL...
BEFORE I CAME HERE...WAS MR. LOGAN HERE?
NO. I DUNNO. WHAT D'Y'MEAN?

ABOVE AND OPPOSITE: WOLVERINE'S RELATIONSHIP WITH MARIKO ENDED TRAGICALLY WHEN HE WAS FORCED TO KILL HIS BELOVED IN *WOLVERINE* #57.

the life of an animal until the Hudsons found him. Windsor-Smith's story served as the basis for the subplot of Wolverine's origin in the second X-Men movie (2004).

Over the years there have been some significant changes in Wolverine's adventures. Writers other than Claremont have tended to stay away from Madripoor as a locale. Logan's romance with Mariko ended sadly when she was poisoned by one of his enemies; in order to put an end to her suffering, Wolverine felt forced to kill her with his claws (*Wolverine* #57, late July 1992).

Shockingly, the X-Men's archfoe Magneto utilized his magnetic powers to extract the adamantium steel from Wolverine's skeleton (in *X-Men* [second series] #25, October 1993). To the amazement of both Wolverine and the readers, he soon discovered that he still had his claws. They were not artificial, as had been widely assumed. Instead, they were made of bone and were the result of his mutations; the Weapon X project had infused them with adamantium as well. So, for a time, Wolverine was considerably more vulnerable than before; until, inevitably, adamantium was again bonded to his skeleton.

SNIKT
FIN

RIGHT: THE SIX ISSUES OF THE ORIGIN MINI-SERIES WERE GATHERED INTO ONE BOOK.

OPPOSITE: THE SHOCKING TRAGEDY OF HIS FATHER'S DEATH CAUSED JAMES HOWLETT'S CLAWS TO EMERGE FOR THE FIRST TIME, REVEALING THAT THEY WERE MADE OF BONE, NOT ADAMANTIUM.

The most significant Wolverine story since the start of this new century has been Wolverine: The Origin, originally published as a six-issue series dated November 2001 through July 2002. This time it was established that the Weapon X project had placed "memory implants" in Wolverine's brain, so that he could not tell which of his memories (before the Hudsons found him) were true and which were false. It was now suggested that Wolverine's healing factor had also affected his mind, suppressing painful memories of the past. The Origin mini-series, co-plotted by Bill Jemas, Joe Quesada, and Paul Jenkins, scripted by Jenkins, and illustrated by Andy Kubert and Richard Isanove, claimed to present the truth about Wolverine's identity and his past.

According to Origin, Wolverine was once a boy named James Howlett, who lived in Alberta, Canada, towards the end of the nineteenth century. The Howlett family was rich and took in a red-headed orphan girl, Rose, to keep young James company. (Various X-Men stories have shown Wolverine to be strongly attracted to his teammate Jean Grey, who also has red hair. Apparently she subconsciously reminds him of his first love.)

But was James really the son of John Howlett? The Howletts' groundskeeper was named Thomas Logan, and, as drawn by Kubert, he looked very much like the adult Wolverine.

It was an awful, revolting noise ~ not a scream, but the birth-cry of a new creature that surely had no place on God's earth.
The thing mewled and whimpered in pain, and those of us who could stand in witness were transfixed ~ both repelled and fascinated by the grotesque spectacle of it.
NN-AHWW... PAPA!
Oh, DEAR GOD.
AWHH... UHH...
AAH! MY HANDS! MY HANDS!

RIGHT: DOG SWORE TO AVENGE HIS FATHER'S DEATH.

OPPOSITE: WHEN ROSE WAS ACCIDENTALLY IMPALED ON HIS CLAWS, LOGAN LOST HIS FINAL TIE TO CIVILIZATION AND VENTURED INTO THE WILDERNESS TO LIVE AMONG THE WOLVES.

After John Howlett fired the groundskeeper, Thomas Logan and his son "Dog" took their revenge by killing him. As James watched the murder, his surge of emotion caused his claws to emerge from his hands for the first time, and he used them to kill the elder Logan.

Horrified by his claws, the Howlett family disowned James as a freak. James and the loyal Rose traveled north, where they found work at a quarry. To conceal James's true identity, Rose dubbed him "Logan." Working at the quarry, Logan proved to be far different than the withdrawn, nonathletic James. Not only did Logan grow much stronger, but an animal-like side of his personality began to emerge. He spent more and more time literally running with the wolves in the surrounding wilderness.

Eventually Dog arrived at the quarry to settle his score with his father's killer. Trying to intervene in their fight, Rose was accidentally impaled by Logan's claws and died. With Rose gone, Logan felt there was no longer anything left to tie him to human civilization, and so he left the quarry for life with the wolf pack.

Today Wolverine continues to be the most popular of the X-Men, appearing in several major X-Men titles as well as his own monthly solo series, numerous mini-series, and an alternate version of X-Men continuity called Ultimate X-Men. He has also been prominently featured in the various X-Men animated television series.

But it was Twentieth Century Fox's two X-Men movies, directed by Bryan Singer, that catapulted Wolverine to a whole new level of fame and popularity. Australian actor Hugh Jackman may be considerably taller than the comic book Wolverine, but his facial features bear an astonishing resemblance to Logan's. More importantly, in his performance Jackman perfectly captured Wolverine's unique personality. With a third X-Men movie planned for 2006, and a Wolverine movie now in development, this Canadian mutant can justly claim a place in the pantheon of the most famous creations in the sixty-five-year history of Marvel Comics.

INDEX

Note: Page numbers in *italics* indicate illustrations.

U

V

W

X

Y

Z

ABOUT THE AUTHOR

Peter Sanderson is a comics critic and historian, and is the author of *Marvel Universe* (Harry N. Abrams) and *The Ultimate Guide to the X-Men* (Dorling Kindersley). Mr. Sanderson earned a BA, MA and MPhil in English literature from Columbia University. Joining the staff of Marvel Comics as an assistant editor, he later became the company's first archivist. In the fall of 2004 Mr. Sanderson began teaching his course "Comics as Literature" at New York University. He currently writes "Comics in Context," a weekly online column on comics, cartoon art, and related subjects at the IGN Comics website, and reviews graphic novels for *Publishers Weekly*. He was an executive producer and co-writer for *Sex, Lies and Super Heroes*, a documentary on comics. He is a consultant for the Museum of Comic and Cartoon Art in New York City. Mr. Sanderson was one of the principal writers for the first four versions of *The Official Handbook of the Marvel Universe*, as well as DC Comics' character encyclopedia *Who's Who*. For more than a quarter century Mr. Sanderson has also written for numerous publications about the comics medium, including *The Comics Journal*, *Comic Buyer's Guide*, and *Back Issue*. Mr. Sanderson lives in New York City.